MW01172159

Dr. Ming Way

BORN RICH LEARN POOR
Vol. 3

Return to Rich

4PM Zen Publishing

4PM Zen Publishing
P.O. Box 867344
Plano, Texas, United States

Printed in the United States of America

ISBN 979-8-9883307-4-5 (paperback)
ISBN: 979-8-9883307-5-2 (e-book)

This book is dedicated to Michael David,
my Essential Observer and Love Bond.

Contents

Rich is a Natural growth experience.

Poor is a Virus conditioned mindset.

— Born Rich Learn Poor

1

Mr. Thorn's Funeral

THE ANIMALS IN the family are closer than ever while fighting in fashion. Polisco has launched his startup venture, which soon turns into a family business. PanRoo, due to her slurred speech, must take an involuntary sabbatical from school. She plays the victim card on the angel investor, Sir Hippono, and successfully becomes the cofounder of the company. Joecub is now a schooler, which turns BarKockalotte into a miserable empty nester. He volunteers to help the master cofounders wherever possible—company security, mail delivery, research, training, and whatnot. And Purrplexy uses her extensive job-hopping and social media experience to land a position in the company as the director of marketing. Family squabbles are embroiled over work snarls, taking the animals to a new level of *togetherness*.

Seemingly, the two seasoned animals—LeDrun and Mr. B.V., serve as executive consultants of the company. Actually, both of Nature's Messengers break their backs to recruit the family for their new Messenger cultivation program on planet F. The dire news is that Nature has only given the program one chance before she must press the reset button, which would eliminate the Social Virus by wiping out all intelligent animals on the gravely infested planet. The good news is that she is now willing to grant them access to the contaminated Life Lab, the I Resort, and the D Lair as training facilities. The sun rises and sets. The moon wanes and waxes. The two Messengers hitherto have made zero progress. The family animals strive to get Rich and escape. They have no interest in saving others.

As the stalemate persists, a deadly prison riot in Star Valley shakes up the situation. Mr. Thorn and his eldest son, the porcupine neighbors across the street, are among the casualties. The porcupine father was killed during his son's visit when the riot broke out. The family, together with LeDrun and Mr. B.V., shows up at the funeral.

THE FUNERAL TAKES place under Mr. Thorn's favorite apple tree by a tranquil pond. They bury the coffins, shed some tears, and erect two spiky tombstones for commemoration. After the sad event, most of the animals disperse. The family sits under the apple tree as the two senior members linger.

"Dad, what is death?" Joecub asks, touching Mr. Thorn's name engraved on the tombstone.

"We have a professional here. Ask him," Polisco answers. He lies on the grass, crosses his stubby legs, and signals the meditating tortoise, the Death Messenger, with his big toe.

"LeDrun," woofs BarKockalotte. He sploots next to Polisco and asks on behalf of Jo, "In your professional opinion, what is death?"

LeDrun slowly opens his eyes, ending his meditation. He gazes at Mr. Thorn's grave and then looks further into the ripples in the pond. After a long while, when Joecub has already forgotten about the question, the Death Messenger begins to chant:

> *life is the beginning of death*
> *death is the beginning of a new life*
> *Love arises at the end of Fear*
> *Fear appears at the consummation of Love*
> *constant the Nature's cycle*
> *unique the Essence of her children*
> *Rich the Essential Legacy*
> *Poor the Viral Legends*

"Are you reciting from our textbook?" asks Mr. B.V., the Life Messenger, who meditates beside the Death Messenger. He opens his eyes to side-eye his chanty buddy and then shuts them back up like a sour sage.

"Hush," LeDrun stealthily shushes Mr. B.V. and continues. "You're a life form—*life* and *form*. Your *life* is endowed in the Origin—Essence, Energy, Love, and Fear. Your *form* is manifested through the eyes of beholders, i.e., Others. Without Essence, you don't have a *life*. Without Others, you don't show your *form*. It is the *natural wholeness of the Self-Other, the art of togetherness*. Remember the Origin I took you to? With regrets?"

LeDrun gives Mr. B.V., the victimized Life Messenger among the family, a guilty glance.

The beaver's eyes stay shut, but his nostrils flare.

"Nature's womb?" PanRoo asks, stroking Purrplexy on her lap. "I remember that place. We met PaGoo there!"

"The juggling boob girl!" Polisco chimes in with his graphic memory.

Mr. B.V.'s face is red and twisted.

"Anyhoo," LeDrun interrupts the insensitive bear couple, "the Origin is where I return your Essence after you die. So, death, in my humble understanding, is putting an end on an otherwise continuous *form*, voluntarily or involuntarily, for a new *life* with a new Essence and a new form."

"It sounds like samsara to me," says BarKockalotte, sitting up on the grass to exhibit a meditation pose. "According to some mystical religions, samsara is an endless circle in which animals …"

"Sam&Sara?" Purrplexy meows, waking up from her nap. "They're the worst cat couple I've ever known on MeowTube. They use their kittens for commercials!"

"According to Mr. Bar," says Joecub under the apple tree, "some cats are female dogs."

"I've never said that," says BarKockalotte. "And not all my words are quotable, buddy, especially those said in bed."

"Life seems like a fool's errand to me," says PanRoo. "We come into life with Essence and then return it after we die, leaving nothing but a pawful of ash. What is the point of living anyway?"

Polisco sniggers. "I wish you still had a slur when you say certain words such as 'ash.'"

"You do leave things to the world besides ash," says Mr. B.V. with a smile.

"I leave a steaming pile to the world every morning,"

Polisco proudly claims while spelunking his right nostril with a chubby finger. "Fresh and sometimes twice!"

"That's inappropriate, Dad!" Joecub coos, frowning at his uncouth father.

"Do you mean the children we leave to the world after we die, Mr. B.V.?" PanRoo, the mother bear, points at her cub climbing the apple tree.

"Maybe yes, maybe no," says Mr. B.V.. "Essential Legacy yes, Viral infection no."

"Then I agree with Pansycakes," says Polisco. "It *is* a fool's errand! Look at Mr. Thorn's life. The thorny guy went to school, found a job, got married, had three kids, lost his wife, and got killed randomly in a prison riot. His diplomas and certificates were torched, bank accounts closed, credit cards shredded, job replaced, everything like *poof!*—gone!"

"I'm sure he will live on in his kids' memories," says PanRoo, looking up at her cub dangling off a branch.

"Memories," Polisco mocks. "Unreliable and overrated. And who knows what he did to the kids behind closed doors?"

"Polisco!" PanRoo yells at the mouthy polar bear.

She chins up to signal Mr. Thorn's grave as if he could still hear them.

"So why do we live then?" asks BarKockalotte, exhaling with sad eyes as he rests his head on his front paws. "I cannot have my own puppies."

"That's the wrong question to ask," says LeDrun to BarKockalotte. "I'm a Death Messenger. I know one thing after animals die: some leave their Legacy that continues enriching other lives while others become Viral Legends that help the Virus infect the coming generations."

"Let's return and be reborn with LeDrun and Mr. B.V.," says Joecub comfortingly to his best friend. "Then I could become a fish or a bird, and you could have puppies."

"I don't care what happens after I die," says Polisco. "I want to get Rich while I'm still alive."

"Well," LeDrun pouts under the apple tree. "Then the Life Messenger may have a better answer for you."

"Ahem!" Mr. B.V. clears his throat with a gloat. "You guys are in luck! We have a cultivation program for new Messengers that ..." He takes out some pamphlets from his bosom and waves them awkwardly to the booing animals.

"Boo! Boo! Booboo!" The animal family is uncharacteristically in accord. "We wanna be Rich! Make us Rich! Fast Rich! Filthy Rich! F Rich!"

The two Messengers exchange frustrated looks. They meditate under the maple tree, silent as tombstones. Slowly, a wicked smile appears on the tortoise's wrinkly face. He nudges his buddy and signals him to look upward at the bear cub.

Joecub is sitting in a tree crotch eating an apple.

LeDrun winks at Mr. B.V., "The cub is the key."

The key drops an apple core and hits the beaver in the front teeth.

2
Jo's Birthday

IT IS THE crack of dawn. Star Valley is in a slumberous trance. In the family's backyard, a squirrel snores in the maple tree, dreaming about a nuts-hunting adventure across the vast backyard terrain. On a branch above the squirrel is a blue jay couple. They play Rock Paper Scissors to decide who will be the noisemaker this morning to wake up the predacious cat in the sunroom. Purrplexy stayed up late for a cyber date with Thoreau last night. She slumbers on her back, showing off her fluffy belly and plum-flower-like paw pads.

"Wuruuuu-tututuutu-hummm—!" Suddenly, a wave of loud noise with violent vibration pierces the idyllic, tranquil morning.

"Holy mother box!" Purrplexy swears in a jolted wakeup. "What the funk is that?"

"Earthquake! Earthquake!" BarKockalotte barks, dragging the sleeping bear cub into the living room.

"Relax," says PanRoo, leaning against her bedroom

doorframe with sleepy eyes and large dark eye circles. "It's Pol's newly upgraded smart lawn mower. Find some earplugs if you want to sleep longer because he also just upgraded the smart vacuum."

"Those upgrades nowadays become more complicated and yet less efficient," Purrplexy yawns. "Sometimes, over smart is worse than plain stupid."

"Says the latter," says BarKockalotte, mocking the cat. "Master Pan, why did master Pol have to get up so early?"

"Because Grandma Ura is coming for Jo's birthday party," PanRoo replies.

"Bam!" The front door is thrown wide open.

"Great! Everybody is up!" Polisco shouts as he walks in, wearing bulky noise-canceling earmuffs. "Let's clean up the house and prepare for the party! I'll grab the vacuum! Grandma Ura is coming to town!"

The bedroom doors slam shut.

A COUPLE OF hours later, the family is up and running. BarKockalotte inflates and bundles the balloons. Polisco stands on a ladder, hanging up some colorful bling-bling decorations around the living room. PanRoo decorates a birthday cake at the dining table while keeping Jo's intrusive little paws from touching the cake. Purrplexy puts her video camera on a tripod and ensures the remote control works.

"Master Pan! Look at the camera!" Purrplexy meows to the mother bear.

PanRoo raises her round head with a scowl.

"Mom!" Joecub screams. "You didn't smile at the camera! That's inappropriate!"

"But my scowl is genuine, my little cake pilferer!" says PanRoo, constraining Jo's creamy little paws.

"What is a birthday, anyway?" asks Joecub, staring at the unattainable cake.

"A birthday is the date you were born," PanRoo says affectionately. "We celebrate it on the same day every year. After the party and the cake, you will be three years old, like another mark of an annual ring inside of a little tree stump. Someday, you will grow into a big tree with many tree rings!"

"If I don't eat the cake," Joecub asks with a puzzled look, "am I still two?"

"You wish," meows Purrplexy. "It is not something for you to decide. There are many ways to make you look younger than your age, though—fillers, Botox, fur transplants …"

"But I'm the boss of everything!" Joecub argues.

"There are things you cannot control, buddy," says Polisco.

"Well," woofs BarKockalotte, backing up his best friend, "according to many physicists and philosophers, the very concept of time is artificial. Age, of course, as a form of temporal measurement, is not …"

Purrplexy interrupts the dog. "Stop talking blah and give me a helium treatment. Thoreau thinks my high-pitched voice is sexy."

"How about an aroma treatment?" BarKockalotte snarls, sitting on the cat's head, wagging his tail.

"Damn it, Stinky!" Purrplexy yowls, wriggling out of the dog's aroma treatment.

LeDrun sits on the top of a red helium balloon and meditates. Disturbed by the pets' hullabaloo, he opens his eyes.

"Jo," says LeDrun, "have you heard the story of a swordsman?"

"No," coos the cub.

"A swordsman was on a boat," LeDrun begins. "The boat was cruising down the river in between high mountains. He enjoyed the beautiful scenery and the smooth ride so much that he took out his sword and started sword dancing. Suddenly, the sword slipped out of his paws and fell into the river."

"What would he do then?" Joecub asks.

LeDrun smiles at the bear cub. "What would *you* do?"

"I would ask Mr. Bar to jump in the river and get the sword!" Joecub replies.

"I would love to, but my vision is still blurry when I look down," whines BarKockalotte.

"I don't care," says Joecub. "I want the sword!"

"There are some things and some animals you want to care about," says Purrplexy.

"Quiet," says LeDrun to the quarrelsome animals. "Joecub is smarter than the swordsman. Instead of retrieving the sword immediately, he took out a small knife and carved the word 'sword' on the boat hull where his sword had dropped. After the boat was docked, he sent good divers to search for his sword beneath the marked area."

"Did they find it?" asks the cub.

"What do you think?" asks Polisco. "The boat moves on, so the mark on the hull becomes meaningless."

"But," woofs BarKockalotte, nervously stealing a glance at PanRoo, "according to master Pan, a birthday is a mark. The number is valid for a whole year."

"That's totally different," says PanRoo. "It is a universal truth that we are one year older after the birthday, celebrating it or not."

"Define 'universal' and define 'truth,'" says LeDrun. "Your life cruises on like a moving boat. The marks are meaningful moments—the sword and the river, the birth and the date, the games and the trophy, the romance and the ring, etc. As the boat moves on, some animals still hold on to the marks and their momentary meanings. Then, they compile them as knowledge and impart it to the next generation. Unlearn. Liberate the Self and save the children."

The tortoise then stands up on the balloon and chants:

Essence cruises, Identity marks
life launches a meaningful journey
Essence inspires, Identity expires
life breathes in rhythm with the universe
Essence interplays, Identity respects
the Self shines through Others
Essence engenders, Identity crafts
Legacy is the cocreation of a masterpiece
Legacy flourishes, Legend narrates
Self-Other togetherness returns to Rich

...

"Pruuufuutulluulu—" Suddenly, LeDrun's sharp claws pierce the helium balloon.

"Rich … a Sanctuar—" LeDrun manages to finish his chant, only to notice his high-pitched squeaky voice. "What happened to my voice? It does not sound wise at all!"

LeDrun struggles among the animals' mocking laughter.

"Your chants usually make no sense to me," meows Purrplexy, stabbing the deflating balloon out of the air with her claw. "But you did say 'Rich' this time. *That* is intriguing."

"I concur," woofs BarKockalotte, inflating another balloon for the tortoise. "I'm a goal-oriented dog. Our first and foremost goal right now is to get Rich and leave the planet. I admire you and Mr. B.V.'s lofty mission to cultivate us as new Nature's Messengers to save the planet from the Social Virus. But a more pressing mission to us is to save ourselves."

"I agree," says PanRoo, putting the birthday cake in the fridge. "I'd love to help other animals, but the planet is completely infested. It only makes sense that we let Nature hit the reset button after we get Rich for the Sanctuary."

"Absolutely!" says Polisco, folding the ladder as he finishes the wall decoration. "Who cares about those suckers and losers? Let them all rot with the Virus!"

"The problem is," says LeDrun, resuming his meditation pose on a new balloon, "you cannot get Rich without Others."

"I don't need nobody!" Polisco roars. "I don't want to save them. They need to save themselves!"

"What about your business?" asks LeDrun. "Do you need customers? And what about him?" The tortoise points his claw at Joecub.

"What do you mean by that?" PanRoo shouts as if the pointed claw pressed a hot button on her.

As the bear couple attacks the tortoise, the doorbell rings.

3
Gifts

G RANDMA URA AND Mr. B.V.'s grandkit wait at the front door. The little beaver points at Ura's wooden food tray in her paws. He faces up with a wide-open mouth, like a baby bird ready to be fed. Smiling, the polar bear grandma shakes her head. She takes two warm garlic fishballs from the food tray and feeds the beaver kit. Meanwhile, Mr. B.V. shuttles between the front door and his van, stacking up four large gift boxes for the birthday cub. The front door opens as he bends over to grab the cultivation program pamphlets and posters in the van.

"Welcome, Mom! Hello Grandma! Hi, Mr. B.V.! …'s butt!" the family greets their guests and their body parts.

"Mom," says PanRoo, taking over Grandma Ura's food tray. "You shouldn't have."

"Oh," says Ura, "the garlic fishballs are PoPo's favorite!"

"Mom!" says Polisco, sniffing the food tray with a frustrated look. "You really shouldn't have!"

"Grandma Ura," Joecub reports to his grandmother, "last time Dad had your fishballs, he sharted in the car!"

"Joecub!" PanRoo gives a stern look at her inappropriate son.

"Where is Thoreau?" asks Purrplexy, looking around to find her lover.

"He was still sleeping when we left," says Grandma Ura.

"He is a dead cat!" Purrplexy hisses.

"Hey! Birthday Boy!" says Mr. B.V. with his signature smile. He finally gathers all his stuff at the front door. "Ready for your birthday gifts?" asks the beaver, patting the gift boxes.

"Yes!" says Joecub with excitement.

"Come on in, everyone!" says PanRoo.

Grandma Ura whispers into Mr. B.V.'s ear: "What does *shart* mean?"

THE PARTY ANIMALS gather around in the living room. Grandma Ura sits on the couch, watching her grandcub chasing and giggling around the gift boxes with BarKockalotte and the beaver kit. Polisco sits next to his mother, mechanically patting the pouty cat while fighting against the urge for his favorite childhood snack that no longer agrees with his digestive system. PanRoo reluctantly directs Mr. B.V. to set up a display rack for the unpopular cultivation program the Messengers keep promoting. LeDrun meditates on the coffee table like a tortoise home décor. Eyes closed. Mouth chewing.

"PoPo," says Ura to her son, "take one. Just one. I baked them this morning. They're still warm."

"No, Mom, no!" says Polisco in anguish. "I've told you a million times I cannot eat them anymore! The boat has moved on!"

"He sharted in the car!" the beaver kit shouts from behind the boxes, copying Joecub's words.

"Hey!" Joecub yells at his beaver friend. "My mom said that's inappropriate!"

"What boat?" Grandma Ura asks Mr. B.V.. "And what is *shart* exactly?"

"*Shards*," says Mr. B.V. with a smirk, "are the ruins of the Social Virus's colonies. LeDrun, would you like to share your wisdom since Fear and Death are your expertise?"

The Life Messenger cues his partner as he struts around the living room and passes his program pamphlets to all adult animals.

LeDrun refuses in a high-pitched cartoon voice. "No."

Mr. B.V. frowns and continues. "Okay. Upon colonization, the red monster builds a Power Center in the victim's Inner Dimension. It is like a headquarters inside the victim that controls and manipulates their Fear Energy. When the colonized body sends out the death signal to the universe through its final and most forceful gasp of Fear Energy, the Virus intercepts the signal, sucks in the Energy, destroys the old Power Center, and spreads to new colonies. The red shards that we Messengers collected on planet **F** for the Social Virus case were nothing but the ruins of numerous destroyed Power Centers."

The proud beaver then clears his throat for his eloquent chanting:

shards are red
colonies are dead
Power Centers are ruined
the Social Virus looks to spread
there is a polar bear cub
he has a bossy dad
the dog

...

"Boo!" Purrplexy shouts from the knoll of Polisco's pot belly. "It is *shart*, not *shard*, you idiot!"

"We have *got* to stop interrupting him when he chants about the dog!" BarKockalotte barks at the cat with deep frustration.

The embarrassed beaver looks at his tortoise buddy for help. LeDrun meditates on the coffee table, eyes closed, mouth chewing, muscles laughing.

"Shart, shard, potayto, potahto," Mr. B.V. mutters with a red face.

"Brahha!" Polisco guffaws. "*Shart* and *shard* are not *potayto potahto* at all! You don't want to get where you shart anywhere near the shards! Brahahah!"

Mr. B.V. changes the subject. "Birthday boy! Ready for your birthday gifts?"

"Hurrah! Yes!" cries Joecub as the animals congregate by the gift boxes.

"These are from me and Mr. B.V.," says Grandma Ura. "A while ago, we talked about my baby grandcub's birthday. I wanted to give him something special, something that he could keep even after I'm gone forever. Mr. B.V. said he could create some great wood-whittling art for Jo. I don't want to spoil it, but brace yourself, these are not ordinary wood-whittling works of art. They are masterpieces. I guarantee you that you've never seen anything like that!"

"Grandma!" Joecub shouts. "I want to open it!"

"Okay, Honey," says Grandma Ura. "Remember, they are from Grandma."

Joecub opens the first gift box.

It is the Loong King Palace—a magnificent red palace with an empty throne, and the bear cub chained to the ceiling of the dungeon.

"Dad! Look!" the startled bear cub shouts. Joecub picks up the Loong Warrior figurine and waves it at his deflated father. "The Loong King Palace! I remembered everything upside down. And you are the Loong Warrior, Dad!"

Polisco bares his teeth at Mr. B.V., then he snatches the Warrior figurine from Joecub's paw and hurls it at the beaver artist.

As if he already foresaw Polisco's violent reaction, Mr. B.V. picks up the meditating tortoise and uses his shell as a shield.

"Bang!" The figurine hits the tortoise shell and breaks into two pieces. One wood piece bounces back to Polisco while the other deflects toward Grandma Ura and hits her in the face.

Joecub screams with gushing tears as he picks up the broken figurine on the floor.

"Polisco!" the angry grandma yells at her son. "What the heck are you doing?"

Polisco stands stiffly, motionless, wordless.

PanRoo picks up her crying cub and comforts him: "Honeycub, look at all your gifts! You wanna open another one?"

"Yes!" says Joecub. His tears transform into a smile as he opens the second gift box.

It is the Hippo Campus—a walnut-shaped campus, two symmetrical seahorse-shaped building complexes, a bald eagle catching the bear cub with her talons.

"Mom! It's your school!" says Joecub with excitement. "ARTISTS IN, PERFORMERS OUT!" Joecub proudly quotes the school slogan.

"Don't say that!" PanRoo roars at the bear cub. "Never say that!"

"But you said that!" Joecub starts crying again. "I was there! Look at me in the bird's claw!"

PanRoo turns to Mr. B.V. with humiliated fury. "What are you trying to do here, Mr. B.V.?"

Mr. B.V. covers his face with the tortoiseshell.

BarKockalotte tilts his dog head and observes the tense situation. He suddenly barks at the allied beaver and tortoise: "Let me take an educated guess. You both turn us inside out and exhibit our Virus to humiliate us. Although I don't understand the cruel intention, I would predict that the next gift box is the Racing City."

BarKockalotte starts unwrapping the third box.

"It's my gift!" the birthday cub shouts at the dog and pushes him away.

Joecub opens the box. As BarKockalotte intelligently deduced, it is the Racing City—the city shaped like stacked onion rings, the red glass headquarters erected on the top, and the raging rodents excavating the foundation at the bottom.

"Mr. Bar with goggles!" Joecub kindly reminds BarKockalotte of his Classopia.

"I don't wear them anymore!"

For the first time ever, BarKockalotte barks at his best buddy.

Joecub grabs a raging rodent and, for the first time ever, attacks *his* best buddy.

BarKockalotte shows his teeth.

"Bark-A-Lot!" says Polisco, holding the charging dog back.

"Joecub!" says PanRoo, picking up her aggressive child.

As the bear couple attempts to cool down the escalated situation, Purrplexy stealthily pushes the last box toward her cat castle.

"Where are you going, kitten?" asks Grandma Ura.

"The sandbox," replies the cat. "I think I know what it is. I have decided to bury the shit."

"But it's mine!" the bear cub squeals from his mom's arms.

Joecub opens the last gift box.

It is nothing but a red wooden box.

The cat is relieved. All the other animals are disappointed.

The tortoise says to the cub: "There is a black button on the bottom. Press it."

Joecub presses the button. The box falls into pieces. A charred two-headed figurine springs out—cat in the front, lioness in the back.

"All ENERGY IN! NO ENERGY OUT!" Joecub quotes Purrplexy's Viral Agent. "Boom! Furless cat!" He then mimics the Box Office explosion.

"My fur's grown back!" Purrplexy hisses at the cub. "Give it to me!" She takes holds the red box and tries to yank it from Joecub's grip.

"No!" Joecub roars. "It's mine!"

As the cat and the cub play tug of war, the rest of the distraught animals attempt to destroy their Viral evidence.

"Stop! All of you!" Grandma Ura maintains order in the clamorous living room. "The gifts are from me and Mr. B.V.! They are wood whittling masterpieces! I want my grandcub to have them as his grandma's legacy. You have no right to destroy these gifts!"

"Mom!" Polisco shouts. "You don't understand! The boat has moved on! Those marks don't mean anything anymore! I hate to be reminded!"

"The boat has moved on," says LeDrun. The tortoise finally regains his wise voice. He levitates in mid-air and continues, "but the sword is still in the water. The Virus's Power Center is crushed, but the shards still glitter. You're on the way to healing, but the child is still infected, thanks to *you, you, you,* and *you.*"

LeDrun's words are like bombs quietly exploding within all of the responsible adults. Joecub's Viral infection has been a family taboo. The adults turn a blind eye to the child's fast-developing infection symptoms because it is too painful for them to sympathetically reflect. Nobody wants to think about it, talk about it or claim responsibility for it. They believe if they all deny it, then it did not happen.

After a long awkward silence, PanRoo says to Mr. B.V.: "Let me see your pamphlet."

4
All Aboard

THE FOLLOWING MORNING, the bear couple quietly sits in bed, like the calm before the storm. PanRoo stares at the pamphlet. Her eyes are fixed on the printed words. Her thoughts about Hippo Campus are racing. Polisco sits next to her, perusing the company's business plan. The blunt tip of the yellow pencil, commanded by his large bear paw, is busy circling and underlining things on the paper. He then rubs the pink eraser on his nose to erase an itch. Each is waiting for the other to fire first.

"We should get Ric—" Polisco pulls the trigger but avoids eye contact.

PanRoo explodes before Polisco can finish his sentence. "What about our cub? I knew I couldn't rely on anybody, especially you!" she says. "I remember that time I couldn't wake you up at midnight to take care of our crying cub. I knew I was all by myself with my baby in this world! I came to this planet with dreams ..."

PanRoo sobs and mourns the dreams of her youth.

"That only happened once!" Polisco lies. "Fine. More than once. It went against my biological clock, for bear's sake! Anyway, that was three years ago! Please don't lapse into your depression again. As for our big upcoming decision, I have thought it through. Hear me out—we need to get Rich and get the fruck out of here before Nature presses the reset button. Let's focus on that."

"How?" asks PanRoo, retracting her tears. "With your impressive business venture portfolio or my teaching experience? The only reason Sir Hippono invested was to shut us up about his secrets in the mansion. And even if we were to succeed purely by luck like lottery winners, what about our cub?"

"What about him?" Polisco asks with self-deception.

"Face it, Polisco," says PanRoo. "He's got the Virus. If we become Nature's Messengers, we could at least save our child. Then we could leave the planet with LeDrun and Mr. B.V.!"

"Our child is fine!" Polisco refuses to admit the truth. "Let's grow the business and get Rich!"

"Gee!" PanRoo mocks. "Are you a polar bear or an ostrich? Get your head out of the sand!"

"Okay," says Polisco, getting off the bed and heading toward the bathroom. "Why don't we present our cases to the board later? But now, I have to piss."

"You're gonna lose!" PanRoo growls.

"Quiet! I'm concentrating!" grunts Polisco from the bathroom.

PLANET F UNDERGOES an unprecedented shortage of everything. Groceries and housing, for instance, are in desperate demand. Rumor has it that the prison riot that killed Mr. Thorn and his eldest son was incited by hungry inmates. It is also quite challenging for the family to find an office space for their business. Under such circumstances, they have turned the sunroom into a home office. It is nine o'clock in the morning. The business meeting starts promptly.

"Um-kum!" Polisco clears his throat while sitting in the power seat at the end of the oval conference table. "Let's begin. Purrplexy, get me some coffee."

"No," says Purrplexy to his left. "We're a flat organization. Nobody is nobody's boss, so you cannot boss me around. Plus, why me? Is it because I'm a female cat? You know I could sue you for discrimination."

"Flat my butt," woofs BarKockalotte, placing a cup of coffee before Polisco. "Someone has to be the lead wolf if we want to achieve anything as a pack, I mean, a team."

"Quiet!" says PanRoo, who sits next to Polisco. "Distinguished consultants," she continues, looking at Mr. B.V., who is sitting at the other end of the conference table, and LeDrun, who meditates on the tabletop in front of the beaver. "Polisco and I have business cases to present about the direction of our company. I had worked hard with everybody to grow the business until yesterday. Joecub's reaction to the birthday gifts made me realize that we've all buried our heads in the sand about his Virus infection. Nobody wants to be blamed for infecting the next generation. I understand. But we cannot turn a blind eye to his symptoms anymore. The last phase of the infection is to kill himself or others. Both will be devastating to the family.

Therefore, I suggest we join Nature's Messenger cultivation program and save the child. That should become our top priority."

"Objection!" Polisco raises his bear paw. "Joecub is fine. We should not divert from heading toward the Rich destination."

"Fine," says PanRoo. "That is why we present the case to the board. Let's vote! Who believes that Joecub is infected?"

PanRoo, LeDrun, and Mr. B.V. raise their paws and claws.

"Purrplexy?" PanRoo asks the cat, whose eyes are on her phone.

"What?" asks Purrplexy. "Can you repeat the question? I was checking email."

PanRoo repeats the question: "Do you think the Social Virus has infected Joecub?"

"I don't know," says Purrplexy with a shrug. "I didn't pay that much attention. Plus, even if I did, I'm not a doctor to diagnose him. So, I abstain."

"Great!" woofs BarKockalotte, who fears voting against either master. "Six votes in total, one abstention. Master Pan wins by majority rule."

"I veto!" says Polisco. "Let's get Rich, and the cub will go to the Sanctuary with us!"

"With the Virus," says Mr. B.V., "he can't."

"And who verified that you adults are completely immune to the Virus?" asks LeDrun in his meditation.

"I thought we won the liberation war?" BarKockalotte woofs, tilting his dog head with confusion.

"The Virus's Power Centers are crushed," says Mr. B.V.. "The Viral shards, however, are scattered about and glittering in every corner of your Inner Dimensions, luring you back into your old Viral habits. Given enough Fear Energy, each shard could swell into a new Power Center for the Virus."

The animals shut their mouths. In quiet introspection, they see glittery red shards lurking in the past and luring them toward the future.

"So," says BarKockalotte, breaking the silence, "there are at least two prerequisites for the Sanctuary—being Rich, and Virus free. Which one is first?"

"Being Rich!" Polisco roars.

"Virus free!" PanRoo roars back.

"I'm the boss!"

"You shart your pants!"

The two cofounders engage in a sophisticated debate.

"Quiet!" LeDrun shouts, opening his eyes and standing up on the table. "Who said that they are two separate things?"

The tortoise walks toward the Power seat and chants:

Essence lives Rich; Virus dies Poor
Rich germinates in Essential connections
Poor infiltrates through Viral relations
Rich grows in Essential environments
Poor infects inside artificial constructs
Rich flourishes in Essential symbiosis
Poor swells via Viral institutions
Rich blooms in offering Essential creations
Poor spreads in meeting Viral expectations
Rich fruits in Essential reciprocities
Poor is decorated by Viral achievements

Essence seeds a new planet
Virus digs graves for unsustainable civilizations

"Rich is having a ton of money," says Polisco, sharing his wisdom.

BarKockalotte butts in to finish his master's sentence. "Poor is the opposite of Rich."

"Ah," Mr. B.V. sighs as he passes the pamphlets around the table. "Relating money to Rich is an excellent topic! I have a poem for you!"

"Nah," LeDrun stops his poetic buddy. "We will address it another time. Today, we want to assure you that by joining our program, you can become Virus free and Rich!"

The animal family looks at one another.

"How long does that take?" asks Polisco, reluctantly browsing the pamphlet.

"One season training," answers Mr. B.V.. "Another season internship."

Polisco frowns. "Too long! Do you have a fast track?"

"Yes," says LeDrun. "We do have a fast-track program. It will consummate before winter comes."

"We do?" Mr. B.V. questions his buddy.

LeDrun gives Mr. B.V. a quick look.

"We do," LeDrun confirms. "But Joecub has to join us. He is the key."

5
Rich Who?

IT IS A drizzling evening. A light fall breeze gently nudges the tiny raindrops into waves and curves, dancing elegantly above the dewy Star Valley. The family's kitchen is warm and bright—PanRoo makes a family-sized pizza, while Polisco puts the clean dishes away from the dishwasher. As he bends over to reach a pot in the lower rack, the polar bear secretly peaks at the panda kangaroo to see if his tempting position gets her attention. PanRoo focuses on making the pizza dough rather than the fluffy bear butt.

"Wonderland!" Polisco bends lower and advertises louder.

PanRoo continues flattening the dough as if she has muted the world around her.

Polisco stands up straight, feeling a little dizzy. He grabs a spatula from the upper rack of the dishwasher and pokes PanRoo's back.

"Knock it off!" says PanRoo.

"What happened to your penis envy?" Polisco asks. "You just missed a golden opportunity to conquer the wonderland."

"Liar," says PanRoo, who knows all her partner's dirty tricks. "You never offer it unless one: you have screwed up something; two: you need something from me; and three: you have gas."

"Nonsense!" Polisco denies, although PanRoo has guessed right about number two and three this time. "I just want to show my affection and wonder if we could have squid ink pizza loaded with fish for dinner rather than just a pizza crust with sprinkles of cheese? I'm so tired of it."

PanRoo sighs. "You should see the grocery stores," she says. "Most shelves are empty. This pizza dough was the last one, and I had to fight for it against many hungry animals."

"Really?" Polisco is surprised. "Let's go out for dinner then. We have money. I have cravings for seafood."

"Everybody has money," says PanRoo, shaking her head. "The **F** government keeps sending us the Virus relief checks and issuing economic stimulus packages. The problem is that everybody has money, but nobody makes things."

"Well," says Polisco, "not everybody has a magic tortoise at home. Why don't we ask the Bulbous Head to conjure some seafood for dinner?"

"It doesn't work that way," says LeDrun, sticking his bulbous head out of the pouch. "I don't mean to intrude in your sweet couple time, but after dinner, could I tell Joecub a bedtime story? I take issue with the stories you two read to Joecub lately. They are quite dark and violent."

"His genius father bought the book," says PanRoo, rolling her eyes.

Polisco defends himself. "He demanded it! He said all his new friends in school admired the supervillain in the book. He felt left out. You should see how he threw a temper tantrum at the bookstore. I will never take him out again!"

"Anyhoo," says LeDrun, "I would like to offer a new bedtime story tonight. You're welcome to join us."

"Do we have a choice?" Polisco asks.

"Not really," LeDrun answers.

JOECUB STILL ENJOYS bedtime stories. His reading interest, however, has evolved from little animals' wild adventures to mean supervillains of mass destruction. After brushing his teeth and combing his fur, the bear cub snuggles with his best canine friend in bed, waiting for another thrilling blowup story. Outside their bedroom door, Polisco slouches against the wall while PanRoo knocks on the door.

"Knock, knock," PanRoo growls.

"Who's there?" BarKockalotte barks.

"Rich Who," LeDrun squeals in the pouch.

BarKockalotte shuts his mouth and signals his buddy to take over.

"Rich Who who?" Joecub shouts.

"Rich Who cocreate Legacy and enrich the Poor!" LeDrun reveals.

BarKockalotte opens the door.

Joecub sits in bed with a pouty face.

"What's wrong, Honeycub?" asks PanRoo, sitting in bed against the headboard and patting the upset bear cub.

"LeDrun tricked me!" Joecub leers at the tortoise, who sticks his head out of the pouch and beams like a happy light bulb.

"He said hoo-hoo," BarKockalotte annotates for his friend.

"What's wrong with hoo-hoo?" Polisco asks with a smirk, sitting on the large brown bean bag on the floor.

"Wee-wee is tough," says Joecub, "hoo-hoo is weak. Tough is good, weak bad!"

"Who told you that?" asks PanRoo, profoundly disturbed.

"Dad!" Joecub points to the brown beanbag.

"I didn't!" Polisco raises his large bear paws to show innocence. "I swear!"

"Mommy," says Joecub, "can you read me another story about the supervillain? He is the best!"

"Why is he the best?" LeDrun asks, crawling out of the pouch and sitting in bed.

"Because he has superpowers!" says Joecub, eyes lit up. "He can roll into a ball—not a regular ball but a super bomb! It blows up a whole city!"

"Isn't he a bad guy?" asks PanRoo.

"All my school friends want to be just like him!" Joecub reasons.

"I see," Polisco comments from the beanbag. "So, you have to change your spots to fit in the gang. Sounds like something your mom would do."

"I wouldn't!" PanRoo raises her voice. "Not anymore!"

"So, what is the story tonight?" BarKockalotte poses

a question to mediate all agitated parties. "Let me grab Purrplexy!"

"She is out on a date, I think," says PanRoo.

"Tonight," says LeDrun with a mystical smile, "the story is about Rich Who."

"What kind of animal is that?" BarKockalotte woofs, tilting his head.

"Can he blow up bigger cities and kill more animals than my supervillain?" Joecub wants to size up this Rich Who.

"You mean who is Rich?" PanRoo reckons. "Definitely not us!"

"Rich Who," LeDrun enlightens the family, "is not a story about What, How, or Why but about Who—the Self and Others, the art of togetherness, the key to a Rich life."

"There is a key?" Polisco is motivated. "Give me the key! Is it to a safe deposit box? Which bank?"

"Rich is not about money," LeDrun rectifies. "It is about your Essence when your life begins and Legacy when your life ends."

"But it is probably measured by money," says PanRoo half-jokingly.

"Only if *you* are measured by money," LeDrun replies. "Rich exits before money. It comes from the Origin. Rich is about Who—Who you truly are, Who you bond with Love, Who reflects your Essence and with Who you cocreate your Legacy. Thus, Rich Who, not How, or moneywise, How Much."

"Bull," says Polisco. "How do you know you're Rich without measuring it with money? You can call yourself whatever you want, but without a ton of money in your bank account, you are just a delusional Poor loser."

"Don't be so harsh on yourself, HoneyPoo," PanRoo teases her partner with cruelty.

"We're in the same Poor boat, HoneySuck," Polisco retaliates.

BarKockalotte howls his allegiance. "I'm in that boat too!"

"My supervillain can torpedo that boat!" Joecub shows off his role model.

Among the animal hullabaloo, LeDrun levitates in mid-air and chants:

Rich is Essential; money is artificial
Rich is natural; money is fiat
Rich lives in Value; money marks the price
Rich is of quality; money is of quantity
Rich is a cocreative process;
money is a measuring tool
Rich inhales to enrich and exhales to nourish;
money inflates into a bubble and deflates into depression
Rich manifests your Essence through Love Bonds;
money calculates your worth with numbers
Rich blooms along your life journey;
money shuttles between destinations
Rich connects to grow;
money transacts to end

"Super bomb! End!" Joecub stands up in bed to give the chanting tortoise a swat.

LeDrun crashes onto the blanket.

"O-u-c-h," LeDrun utters a slow moan as he is stranded on his shell.

"So, what is the story tonight?" PanRoo asks, confining the cub in her arms.

LeDrun takes out his purple crystal flask from inside the shell and guzzles up. He looks at the ceiling and commands: "Paws on my chest button. Time to return to the Lab."

6
Return to the Life Lab

THE ANIMALS OPEN their eyes in a dimly lit Lab. Red rays creep through the cracked window glass to glitter on well-organized tubes and flasks, beakers and burners, microscopes and scales, and on two busy lanky shadows. The taller shadow wears a coat. He moves in a circle while juggling two flasks like a wizard dancing a wicked dance. The flasks glow in the dark—one green and the other purple, intermingling with the red rays from outside to portray the inner turmoil of the infected animals. The smaller shadow appears to be a cat. She sits on the countertop and spectates the circus act. Her head moves around, following the trajectories of the flasks. LeDrun signals the family to keep quiet. He stealthily levitates around the juggling shadow and pauses before his eyes.

"Hey, buddy!" LeDrun suddenly shouts at the dancing shadow and grins like a child.

Startled, the shadow drops the purple crystal flask. "Holy mother f—nature!" he swears.

LeDrun lands on the countertop next to the cat. The tortoise then snaps his fingers to turn on the lights. The Lab instantly brightens up. Strong light attacks all the animals' eyes and makes them squint. After they are accustomed to the new lighting, the animals find an angry beaver and a grumpy cat.

"Mr. B.V.?" Joecub asks nervously, paws behind his back. "What are *you* doing here?"

"This is my Lab, remember?" says Mr. B.V.. "Ah, how I miss the simple life!"

"What Lab?" PanRoo asks.

"The Life Lab," LeDrun answers. "The one you guys have contaminated with the Virus."

"Nah," Polisco shakes his head. "I remember that Lab vividly. It is a greyish place. Everything is a blur there except the juggling boo—, I mean, the Life Messenger."

"That's me!" says Mr. B.V., scowling at the family. "Anyway, thanks to the Virus, this is what the Life Lab looks like now."

The guilty animals look around the Lab. They see glass containers of various shapes, colors, and sizes that are clearly cataloged, labeled, and coded. The containers are neatly placed from top to bottom on countless tall shelves parallel to one another. The tall and solemn shelves line up alphabetically in their respective categories, classes, and subjects. The animals are in awe.

"Wow!" BarKockalotte howls. "It is like a magnificent library! A baby lab and library!"

"Ugh!" Purrplexy yowls at the dog. "That sounds horrendous! Plus, there are no babies anywhere to be found!"

"Why are you here?" BarKockalotte barks at the cat. "I thought you had a date."

"Damn Thoreau wanted to play video games together," says Purrplexy. "As I was bored to death, Mr. B.V. joined the game online and messaged me in private saying that he had a better place to go. I followed his lead and ended up here. Am I still in the game? I'm quite perplexed."

"Ladies and gentlemen," Mr. B.V. announces, raising his voice, "welcome to our Messenger cultivation program! I am the Life Messenger PaG—well, you can call me Mr. B.V., and that is the Death Messenger LeDrun!"

The Life Messenger introduces the Death Messenger on the countertop.

"Un-kum!" LeDrun clears his throat and stands tall. "Welcome, future Messengers! Tonight, we have our first class—Born Rich. This is where you were born, so …"

"You're a genius!" Polisco shouts with excitement. "I knew signing up for your program was a good idea. *We were born Rich*! How come it has never occurred to me? The secret place is our birthplace! So, where is the money?"

BarKockalotte helps with his extensive library experience. "Check the catalog!" he woofs. "It is alphabetical. Find the letter P down the aisle, master Pol!"

"Hold on," says Mr. B.V.. "The fact that you were born Rich has nothing to do with money but with your Natural ability to co-survive and cocreate with all lives because you are all Nature's children. It is the Virus that separates you and turns you against each other. The cultivation program helps you revive that inborn aptitude for a Rich life experience. Now, I want you to close your eyes and return to the Origin."

The animals close their eyes.

After a while, BarKockalotte starts snoring.

"Mr. Bar!" LeDrun yells at the sleeping dog.

"What? What!" BarKockalotte opens his dazed eyes, then he falls asleep again.

"I recall," says PanRoo, "the Origin is a greyish ball of goo. There are no discernable shapes, forms, colors, sounds, or whatnot, but LeDrun said everything comes from it."

"Yes!" BarKockalotte wakes up once more to support his master. "According to LeDrun, the Origin has all the life Essence that contains endless potentialities, and it also contains life Energy that constantly moves around and about."

"What about the two Magic Powers?" asks Mr. B.V., waving the green crystal flask while searching for the lost purple one on the floor.

Joecub subconsciously touches his pocket like a little thief.

"Love and Fear," says Polisco, "the two Magic Powers we are endowed with from the Origin. The green one contains Love that attracts; the purple one contains Fear that repels. Love guides us to discover our Essence; Fear guards us along the journey. But I don't care about the journey. Where is the damn money?"

"No, no, no," says Mr. B.V., shaking his head. "Money is not part of Nature's design. Thus, it has nothing to do with your Essence when you are alive nor Legacy after you die. It is a medium that intelligent animals use for economic exchange. The **F** money circulated in the **F** society is problematic. It does not hold intrinsic Value, nor is it backed up by real commodities with Energy. Rich engenders from your Essence and grows when your Love bonds with Others. It is the natural circle of growth, like tree rings, if you will. Money, however, has nothing to do with organic growth. It is just a medium and a measurement. As for the **F** money you are all obsessed with, unfortunately, is an unsustainable make-believe."

"Nonsense," says Purrplexy. "When we talk about Rich folks, like Sir Hippono, money is the only gauge. Who cares what kind of animals they are?"

"Money has Power," says PanRoo. "And no one on planet **F** can live without it. I agree with Pol that in order to be Rich, we need to have a ton of money and zero Virus. Then we can go wherever we desire—the Sanctuary, in our case."

"What if the **F** money contains the Virus Code that spreads?" asks LeDrun.

"I love money!" Joecub takes sides with his parents.

Mr. B.V. frowns. He sighs and turns to LeDrun: "Is it too late to find new disciples?"

LeDrun gazes at the shelves of organized red jars, then smirks at the animals.

"Do you want to see your entire life?" LeDrun asks as he points to the shelves. "The Life Lab stores all life trajectories like movies. Locate your jar and look into it."

The unleased animals plunge into the towers of shelves and fanatically search for the jars that contain their life movies. Mr. B.V. and LeDrun sit on the countertop and clink their crystal flasks.

After a while, the animals return with their heads hanging down. They sit on the floor, thinking, pondering, staring into space. Joecub is confused about what he saw. He chins up toward the two Messengers on the countertop.

"I watched a movie in the jar," says Joecub. "I'm the star in it."

"What did you see?" Mr. B.V. asks with a smile.

"A lot of things!" Joecub gets excited. "I'm a supervillain bear—red chair, numbers, bull, bald eagle, toys, guns and stuff. But in the end, I disappear. My parents and Mr. Bar are crying. Why do they cry? Am I dead?"

Joecub turns around and looks at his family.

Polisco remains quiet. PanRoo starts weeping.

"We're all freaking dead! One after another!" Purrplexy swears. She then yells at the two Messengers: "Why are you scaring us? We're not going to die like that, are we?"

LeDrun smiles graciously. "It is up to you," he says. "How you live is up to you, and so is how you die. What you just saw is a scenario of your life and death through the prism of your belief, the belief that being Rich equals having lots of money. You give Power to something in the middle between the Self and Others, then you break your life in half. Everything is prescribed toward money as the goal, and the rest of your life after reaching the goal is your struggle to keep it and the pain of losing it. In other words, your life ends in the middle."

"And the Virus is in the middle," woofs BarKockalotte.

"So," says Polisco, "you said that the horrible things we saw in the jars are just a life- and-death possibility based on what we think. What about other possibilities? Can you conjure a happily-ever-after one for us?"

"We can't," says Mr. B.V., "but *you* can. Every thought

generates a potentiality. Changing what you think will change your life trajectory."

"How?" Polisco asks with a scowl.

"Well," Mr. B.V. beams, "you are in luck! Our step-by-step cultivation program not only helps you return to Rich but also to the Sanctuary!"

LeDrun joins the marketing pitch. "Because they are one and the same."

"What is the first lesson?" PanRoo cannot wait.

"To bring you here and scare yo—" Mr. B.V. bites his tongue as his buddy shuts him up with eye contact.

"Unlearn what the Virus has taught you," says LeDrun.

7
What Goes Up

POLISCO AND HIS delinquent son are kicked out of the principal's office. The father bear's loud threat to sue the school for traumatizing his child reverberates throughout the hallway, gushes out, and blows some feathers off of a couple of birds in a tree. After getting in the car, Joecub has to remind his roaring father that the principal probably cannot hear him anymore. When Polisco furiously drives his car and his frightened cub home, the rest of the family members gather in the living room for the details of the news.

"How did it go?" PanRoo asks, opening her arms to the cub.

"Suspended," Polisco replies, kicking off his round leather shoes.

"What?!" PanRoo raises her voice. She pushes Joecub away from her chest, holds his shoulders, looks into his eyes, and asks: "What did you do exactly?"

"I didn't do anything!" Joecub denies. "It was Dad! He threw a ball at the principal!"

"It was not my fault," says Polisco on his way to the fridge for a beer. "There was a stress ball on his desk. And I didn't like the way he talked about our son, so."

"Honeycub," PanRoo gives a side-eye to Polisco, holds Joecub's little paws, and asks, "Why did you fight with your new bull calf friend at school?"

"Because of the seesaw," says Joecub with a frown. "I liked being up, but he kept bringing me down! I told him to keep me up all the time because I'm the boss. He laughed at me. So, I pushed him. He pushed me back. I hit him. He hit me back. Then the teacher came."

The adult animals stare at Polisco, the source of the "I am the boss" infection.

"Well," woofs BarKockalotte, "I understand that being up is better than being down, but there has to be give and take in the seesaw situation."

"Why?" Joecub asks with dissatisfaction.

"Because you two share a beam," says PanRoo. "That you are always up makes him always down. I understand that you do not want to be laughed at by your friend. It is a horrible feeling! But pushing and hitting him is never a good idea."

"I don't understand," meows Purrplexy. "If you wanted to be up all the time, climb onto a tree or the roof of a building and stay there. I climb to the top of my castle and stay there all the time, especially when BarKockalotte barks. Why did you play seesaw?"

"I like *going up*!" Joecub raises his arms to illustrate the movement of ascending.

Purrplexy looks up and sighs. "Like a rising star," she purrs. "I understand that desire. But every sunrise is followed by a sunset, not to mention that there is a connection between your rise and his fall."

"I don't know the connection," Joecub shouts. "But I'm the boss!"

"Dude," says Polisco with a sigh. "I understand you want to be the boss so you can control the situation. I have been there. But there are many things you cannot control, such as the physics of a seesaw."

Joecub throws himself onto the floor and starts screaming. The bear cub's world-class tantrum shakes all of Star Valley and makes the setting sun flinch.

The adults shake their heads. They look at LeDrun, who meditates on the large coffee table, eyes closed. Purrplexy sticks her paw out and pokes the tortoise for a solution. Agitated, LeDrun's face wrinkles up. He opens his eyes, slowly crawls toward the squealing bear cub, and whispers something into his ear. Enchanted, Joecub turns off his tantrum and turns on a smiley face, like a blooming sunflower after a thunderstorm.

"What did you tell him?" BarKockalotte woofs with curiosity.

"The Love Balloons," says LeDrun with a wink. "He likes ascending, doesn't he?"

LeDrun smiles, signaling everyone to gather around him.

"It is a trap! I am not going!" Purrplexy yowls as she painfully recalls how the Love Balloon ejected her into a sky dive last time.

BarKockalotte dislodges the cat's claws from one of the coffee table legs and makes her join the gang.

THE ANIMALS OPEN their eyes on the top floor of a skyscraper. Through the large window walls, they see hazy smog blurring the horizon. A big dam is stretched across a winding river, like a serpent cut in half. Numerous tall buildings and construction sites line up along the river-banks. Honking cars, colorful flashing lights on emergency vehicles, shrieking police sirens, pepper spray and tear gas spice up the civilization party.

"Where are we?" BarKockalotte barks from behind Polisco. "Downtown Star Valley? I hate downtown!"

"I thought you said Love Balloons," Purrplexy meows from behind BarKockalotte. "Where is the Resort?"

"Love Balloons!" Joecub shouts. "I want them now!"

"Ladies and gentlemen," says LeDrun, levitating in midair. "Welcome to the I Resort!"

"Boo!" Polisco courteously expresses his disagreement. "We have been to the I Resort. It is like a Nature's marvel, not a development disaster!"

"He's right," says PanRoo, looking around in search of her memories. "The Resort I remembered had emerald mountains, sapphire lakes, velvet grass valley, and a giant sequoia tree."

"I remember the entrance to the tree!" barks BarKockalotte. "The tree had a knot on its trunk. Last time, master Pol pressed it, and we arrived at the magical brisé-fan-shaped Love Terrace where our Love Balloons picked us up for wondrous journeys. Where is everything?"

"Chill, guys!" LeDrun shouts with slight frustration. "This is what the I Resort looks like after the Social Virus contamination, all right? Do I need to remind you how this pristine retreat was contaminated in the first place?"

"*You* took us here," Polisco mumbles defensively.

LeDrun glances at the polar bear and continues: "The elevator is that way. Follow me. Mr. B.V. is meeting us out on the Love Terrace."

The animals file into the luxurious hallway with multi-dimensional LED screen walls, on which commercials constantly pop up with dazzling colors, blaring music, and promising slogans. Joecub is so mesmerized by the LED screens that Polisco must carry him into the elevator. Unsurprisingly, the whole elevator is just a cuboid-shaped hallway where commercials on the LED screens move up and down. Finally, the exhilarated cub and the overstimu-lated adults arrive at the Love Terrace. The vast, hazy sky is filled with balloons of various sizes, shapes, and colors. All the gondolas hanging below the balloons are made of LED screens that strive to convince you that you would love the balloon trips they have designed and planned for you. To the left of the elevator, a large touchscreen plays a demo video that repeatedly shows how the platform works.

"There you are!" Mr. B.V. greets the gang with his signature smile. "Ready for another cultivating session?" he asks, rolling up his sleeves. "As a Life Messenger and a Love expert, I'm telling y—"

"I want balloons!" Joecub yells at Mr. B.V.

"Mr. B.V.," says PanRoo, "this is not the I Resort we

remember. Last time we were here, it was serene and idyllic. We meditated on the terrace and attracted our respective Love Balloons. What is this in front of us? An obnoxiously aggressive balloon market? We want to go back to our Love Balloons like last time."

Purrplexy pouts. "Speak for yourself."

"Master Pan!" BarKockalotte woofs with tongue-hanging excitement. He stands before the touchscreen and says: "Check out the interface! There are millions of balloon trip offers! Each page has pictures, package info, and costs. And you can swipe to pick! Right swipe to give it a bone symbol to pick and left swipe a fire hydrant!"

"Sounds like the interface can recognize your dog face," says Polisco with a smirk.

"Sounds like an outdated dating app to me," Purrplexy yawns.

"LeDrun!" Mr. B.V. calls for support. "I told you it was a bad idea to bring them here. Look around! How am I supposed to cultivate their Love when there are millions of things here to steal their attention?"

"Relax," says LeDrun to his frustrated teaching partner. "We cultivate with what we have." The tortoise turns to the loud animals and says: "Listen up! Ignore all the attention hogs around you. Even though the Social Virus has contaminated the Resort, the monster cannot get to you if you do not give it your Energy. Now, I want you all to close your eyes and meditate. When your Fear ebbs and Love flows, the wave will attract your Love Balloon, like you did last time."

The animals remain quiet for two seconds.

"I don't think so," says Purrplexy. "Last time, that damn

Love Balloon almost killed me. There is no way I'll go back to that!"

"She's right," BarKockalotte agrees. "I'd rather not go back to the doghouse that keeps bouncing up and down. It's exhausting."

"Love attracts many possibilities," says LeDrun with a smile. "If you just close your eyes and ..."

"Can Love attract a Rich life for us?" Polisco asks.

"Of course!" Mr. B.V. beams proudly. "The more Love attracts, the Richer you become, get it?"

Hearing Mr. B.V.'s words, the financially motivated adults waste no time and start meditating. The children follow suit. The two Messengers whisper to each other and snigger. After quite a while, Polisco opens his eyes and runs his mouth. "That didn't attract jack shit."

"What's your number?" PanRoo asks, intending to compare notes.

"A billion," says Polisco. "You?"

"Not enough," says PanRoo. "Sir Hippono is probably worth several billion, yet he is still on this infested planet. The Sanctuary requires way more, for sure. With the crazy inflation and all, I was thinking a trillion dollars."

"Mine is one sextillion," says Purrplexy. "The number is simply bigger and sexier. How about you, Bark-A-Lot?"

"Umm, I'm still calculating," says BarKockalotte. "And for the last time, the emphasis of my name is on the letter 'K'!"

"Where is my balloon?!" Joecub shouts with an upset face.

The adults look at LeDrun. LeDrun looks to Mr. B.V..

"Um-kum!" Mr. B.V. clears his throat and exhibits his

front teeth. "You are all applying it wrong. The Law of Attraction applies to your Love, *not* money."

8
Law of Attraction

POLISCO IS DEEPLY disappointed. He sits on the brisé-fan-shaped Love Terrace and looks beyond the two Messengers. Numerous balloons float through the air, promising him that everything is within arm's reach. However, he is told to close his eyes, clear his mind, and let his Love attract and guide. Nothing happens. When Mr. B.V. talks about applying the Law of Attraction to life experiences but not to money, Polisco explodes.

"Bullshit!" says Polisco, interrupting Mr. B.V.'s teaching. "The stupid meditation didn't work. You know what it attracted? Numb legs!"

PanRoo realizes something. She holds Joecub in her arms and says to Polisco: "Let's not get sidetracked. We signed up for the program to save the cub. Then we can get Rich and go to the Sanctuary together."

"Fine!" says Polisco, frowning at Joecub. "I have one last question: Why in the hell can't we attract money? Don't you want to get the training and enriching done all at once? Time, speed, efficiency. Come on guys!"

LeDrun nods and smiles at Mr. B.V..

Mr. B.V., the Life Messenger and Love expert, takes a deep breath and begins: "Naturally, the Origin is brimming with life Essence and Energy. Essence is unique, while Energy is universal. Unique, so each life is a novel artwork. Universal, so all lives are interconnected as one. Your unique Essence always merges with the universal symbiosis whenever you let it shine. To help you along the journey, the Life Lab empowers you with Love and Fear— the two Essential Forces of interaction. Love is the Force of Attraction, Fear Repulsion. Open to attract. Close to repel. Open to bond, bond to enrich, enrich to grow. Close to mark, mark to define, define to show. Attraction and Repulsion are in a dynamic balance within and without. You grow Rich as you experience and cocreate along the symbiotic journey. And you were born with everything you need for a Rich life experience. In other words, you were BORN RICH. Poor, however, is a Viral mindset that separates the ..."

Polisco interrupts. "Quit the nonsense. Just tell me why we cannot attract money. We love money. Love attracts. Perfectly logical!"

"Maybe because we cannot directly experience money?" PanRoo says.

Purrplexy disagrees. "Of course we can experience money," she purrs. "Look at all the balloons in front of us! They all promise great experiences at varying costs."

"That's still not experiencing money directly," woofs BarKockalotte, backing up his master Pan. "It may buy experience, but money itself is not experience. According to Mr. B.V., Rich is in the experience. Therefore, money is *not* synonymous with Rich."

"You're synonymous with ridiculous," Purrplexy mutters. "If having sextillions of **F** money is not Rich, what is, huh?"

"**F** money is the worst!" barks BarKockalotte. "It is not even backed by real things!"

"Are you saying that the Power of the **F** government is not real?" asks Polisco, raising his eyebrow.

Among the animal quarrels, LeDrun levitates up like a tortoise balloon in mid-air. The Death Messenger then chants:

> *Love attracts to grow, Fear repels to show*
> *the Virus disguises Fear as Love*
> *Love engenders, Fear measures*
> *the Virus disguises increase as growth*
> *Love produces, Fear calculates*
> *the Virus replaces productivity with numbers*
> *Love shares, Fear transacts*
> *the Virus replaces connections with transactions*
> *Love fulfills, Fear finishes*
> *the Virus equals Value to price*
> *Love enriches, Fear accumulates*
> *the Virus fabricates a money fiction around Rich*

As the tortoise chants on and on, Joecub catches sight of a balloon that promises a supervillain trip. Captivated, the bear cub escapes his mother's arms and jumps off the terrace for the promise. Instinctively, PanRoo tries to grab the cub but loses balance herself. The mother bear hangs off the high terrace of a skyscraper with one paw, and the other paw tightly grasps her cub. Polisco hurries to the rescue, but they are too heavy for the fluffy polar bear.

"HELP! HELP!" BarKockalotte howls as he pulls on Polisco's belt to aid the rescue.

"Polisco," LeDrun shouts, "close your eyes and think of what you Love. Like last time. The Love Balloon will save all of you."

Polisco's mind goes blank. He closes his eyes and concentrates. His dream office emerges in his mind. At the speed of thought, a monument-shaped Balloon with two adjoined igloos appears and picks up the endangered animals.

"Now what?" Mr. B.V. asks LeDrun, who watches the Love Balloon floating away.

"Let's meet them at the next stop," says LeDrun with a smile.

THE ANIMALS ARE in Polisco's dream office. Frosty walls are decorated with vision boards, business growth charts, roadmaps, and slogans. Icy cubicles are filled with typing robots with happy family pictures and snacks. The aroma of seafood permeates the air of the company cafeteria, where a giant snowbear resembling Polisco stands on a motorized rotating pedestal at the center of the floor. The executive's office is roomy and bright. Sitting on a soft loveseat by the wall windows, the animals look out over an outdoor snowball stadium where the crowd watches a game, drinking and chewing with their loudmouths.

"This is it!" PanRoo acclaims. "I remember your dream office! And the soft loveseat."

"It is a super cool place, master Pol!" BarKockalotte howls.

"It's cooler than cool," meows Purrplexy. "It's cold!"

"The perfect temperature for a polar bear!" Polisco grins. "Come on! I want to show you the conference room."

"Where is Mr. B.V.?" Joecub asks, looking around for his friend.

The adult animals realize that the two Messengers are not with them.

"Perfect!" says Polisco. "No nagging. Let's get down to business!"

The animals sit down in the conference room. On the whiteboard behind him, Polisco writes down his dream product—the cheerleader robot.

"I remember your cheerleader obsession," says PanRoo, rolling her eyes.

"It's not an obsession," says Polisco. "It is my deepest passion from my core, my Essence! Together, let's make the dream come true!"

"Why cheerleader robots?" Purrplexy asks. "I was a cheerleader for a wildcat team once. It was not as glamorous as it appeared, except the parties and sex."

"Our product is one of a kind," says Polisco passionately. "When I was in high school, I was in a band called Bear Lords. I will never forget a gig we played, when our crowd sang along and gave us our very first ovation. The joy was immense and overwhelming like a wave having found its ocean. A profound resonance with others made me cry with joyful tears. I've never felt that way since, not even at my wedding. Please don't take it the wrong way, Pansycakes. On planet **F**, we all focus on ourselves. Nothing is wrong with that, but our product could bring balance because they cheer for others. Our cheerleader robots all have AI-powered world-class empathy and compassion. They cheer you up to pursue your dreams!"

Polisco's passionate speech touches everyone's heart. The motivated animals loudly discuss how they can contribute to the cocreation of the product.

"I'm an excellent researcher," says PanRoo. "I can study the market and potential customers with surveys, questionnaires, and big data."

"I can take care of customer service," woofs BarKockalotte. "I take pride in serving other animals."

"I'll devise a killer marketing strategy," meows Purrplexy. "I have connections in show business."

"All right," says Polisco with excitement. "I'll develop the product with a crack tech team."

The animals then huddle together like a professional sports team.

Meanwhile, in the airborne world outside, the Love Balloons of his endeavoring teammates have somehow come together to form a bouquet with Polisco's Balloon in the center. Three gondolas encircle Polisco's, suspended just above it, with one hanging from a leaf-shaped Balloon in sage green, another from an orange fuzzy ball-shaped Balloon, and one beneath a box. Three inflated arms reach down into the igloo's windows from the other gondolas, like three evacuation slides on an airplane. The bonded Love Balloons twirl together, arm-in-arm, toward cloud nine.

In a blink, the company releases their product. Polisco stands in front of an LED screen wall, hosting the company's first product launch event. The polar bear entrepreneur introduces the new product with deep pride and passion. All of his Love Bonds—PanRoo, BarKockalotte, and Purrplexy—applaud with tears in their eyes. After the product is released to the market, the bouquet of bonded Love Balloons slowly descends. The product embodies their unique Essence, together with their Love-charged Energy. Like a ripe fruit, the innovative cheerleader robot sends out an invitation to attract those who naturally resonate with the Essential Message it carries.

In another blink, the company has become public. The animals sit in the conference room for the interim progress report. Polisco stares at the report with a solemn face. Everyone else is silently preparing their defenses.

"We barely made a profit," says Polisco, staring at the report.

"Who cares?" says Purrplexy. "Our market value is really high. As long as they continue investing in us and buying our stocks, I am fine with making no profits."

"I care!" says Polisco, raising his voice. "We must do a better job growing the business. There is still some time before we have to issue the annual report to the public. I will not accept a loserly report. Pan, what are your findings?"

"Well," says PanRoo with a frown, "the market is not responding positively. We have negative reviews of the product as well as customer service. The brand value is negligible compared to the cost of marketing and PR."

"Our marketing strategy is top-notch," says Purrplexy. "I cannot make a lame product shine."

"We have the most intelligent engineers," says Polisco. "Maybe we should cut the budget on all overhead and unprofitable departments to focus on product development."

"Master Pol," whines BarKockalotte, "we already use third-party vendors for customer service. They are extremely budget-friendly, but we cannot always ensure the quality. And, in my humble opinion, we shouldn't squander money on marketing while skimping on customer service."

"It's time to set some goals and deadlines," says Polisco.

"I can come up with some KPIs for each department," says PanRoo. "You know, numbers do not lie."

As the company animals point fingers and bare their teeth, the arms adjoining the gondolas disconnect from each other and begin descending like a plane ready for a rough landing.

"I hate going down!" Joecub cries out.

In a split second, the Balloons touchdown on a lake. Polisco's phallic igloo-shaped Love Balloon transforms into a semi-transparent, membrane-like Fear Bubble. Next to his are three other Fear Bubbles. The dog, the cat, the panda kangaroo, and the bear cub are enwrapped respectively. Outside the Fear Bubbles is a larger Collective Fear Bubble that envelops them all. The Fear Bubble submerges halfway beneath the water surface, leaving the other half of the sphere bobbing up and down with the waves.

9
Law of Repulsion

THE FEAR BUBBLE floats on a lake of a desert oasis. The desert is highly commercialized. Buildings with various architectural styles and cultural symbols line up like a strip mall. Dazzling LED lights on the buildings and billboards, fretful streetlights and impatient headlights vie for attention, driving away the peaceful darkness of the night sky to shroud the stars.

"Should we take a break?" asks PanRoo from within her Fear Bubble. "It's getting late."

"I could use a drink," meows Purrplexy from her Bubble. "I bet I can find a fabulous cat club along the strip mall."

"Concentrate!" says Polisco. "Do you see the numbers on that whiteboard? They are your key performance indicators. Focus on achieving them on time. Those who fail their KPIs are not qualified for the bonus program. Those who fail twice will be removed from the board. The deadline is coming up!"

The anxious animals quietly stew inside their Fear Bubbles and work hard on achieving their separate goals. Meanwhile, another Fear Bubble launches its voyage from the shore. Inside it are a wise tortoise and a joyful beaver. Their Bubble encircles the animals' Collective Fear Bubble, but it cannot get close enough to dock due to a repulsive force that pushes it away. The two Messengers discuss and then meditate. In a split second, another Fear Bubble emerges from inside the lake with a prominent brand logo and company name imprinted on it. Working like a charm, the Messengers' Fear Bubble is pushed farther and farther away from the new rival Fear Bubble and closer and closer to the animals' until it finds its way in.

"Long time no see!" says Mr. B.V. with a big smile.

"Welcome to my big **D** Lair!" LeDrun, the proud host, opens his arms to the stressed-out guests.

"Bear Lord!" "Holy box!" "Son of a female dog!" "What did you say?" The preoccupied animals are startled by the interrupting voices and confused by their words.

"This is not the **D** Lair," says Polisco. "I remember that damn place. It was a glass boo—I mean a dome building with lots of crazy purple lightning."

"Yes," PanRoo agrees. "You sat on a pedestal and waited to receive death signals."

"They lit you up like a torch!" BarKockalotte barks.

"The haunted house with many doorways to death?" meows Purrplexy with flattened ears. "I hated that place!"

"I love bubbles!" Joecub recollects the fun memories of blowing bubbles with LeDrun.

"What else do you remember, Polisco?" asks LeDrun, smiling at the brightly and colorfully lit offshore desert.

"You mean the desert?" Polisco raises his eyebrow. "It had nothing but snakes, insects, and hyenas!"

"It did have an oasis," PanRoo reminds her partner-in-crime. "Those hyenas lived by the lake."

Polisco nods his fluffy head. "Yeah. Those nasty animals. But there were two lakes. Like the devil's eyes, bottomless inferno. What happened to the other lake? Got pirated?"

"Nope, got landfilled," says LeDrun with a pouty face. "Thanks to your visit, the Virus has spread throughout the Lair. Two tribes of gamblers, led by a bear and a bull respectively, have occupied the desert. They fight constantly—the bear wants to go up, so does the bull. When the bear goes up, it becomes bull, and the bull becomes bear."

"Bear bull, bull bear," Mr. B.V. concludes.

"It sounds like they are playing a seesaw," BarKockalotte woofs with a tongue-hanging smile at Joecub.

"I want to go up!" Joecub shouts. "The bad bull keeps me down!"

PanRoo turns to LeDrun "What is your point?" she asks. "The desert is way over there. We somehow ended up in the lake. Where is the Love Balloon? How is it possible that it turned into a Fear Bubble? Can we go back up in the Balloon, please? I like it there much better."

"Ah, the Law of Repulsion," says LeDrun, inhaling profoundly to utter his chant.

"Wai-, wai-, wait," says Mr. B.V., stopping the wise tortoise. "Let me try. I've prepared for this one." Then the beaver shares:

the bear cub wants to go up
and always up
his fat father has a dream

63

he measures it in altitude with his poop team
so Love becomes Fear
they set up measurements loud and clear
near the Fear Bubble the Virus lurks
dreamland the Virus tempts
a colony in disguise
the dog …

"What do you mean 'poop team?'" PanRoo demands, interrupting the poetic beaver. "We're a dream team!"

"A fat father?" Polisco growls. "For the last time, I'm not fat. This is my natural build!"

"Wait," says Mr. B.V.. "The climax, the Law of Repulsion!"

"My partner," says LeDrun to the beaver, "leave it to the Fear expert. We're in my Lair, after all." The Death Messenger squeezes out of his Fear Bubble, levitates, and chants:

Love attracts, Fear repels
Law of Attraction, Law of Repulsion
Love opens up to attract something out in the universe
Fear closes up to repel everything nearby
Love sends out invitations and receives resonance
Fear sends out rejections and results in loneliness
Love attracts experiences with direction and intensity
Fear repels the surroundings with recoil and backfire
Love attracts at the speed of thought
Fear repels with Energy-consuming action
Law of Attraction generates waves of possibility
Law of Repulsion draws the boundaries of certainty

"Great lecture," says Polisco, brushing off the enthusiastic teacher. He takes out some cash and thrusts it into the tortoise's shell like a generous client at a strip club. "Go ahead. Have some fun gambling. It suits your age. We have real business to do here."

"Real?" Mr. B.V. raises his voice, clearly offended by the polar bear. "You tell me what is real right now!"

"Chill! Geez," says Polisco defensively. "Well, we have a real product line—the cheerleader robots. I lead the development team, thank you very much. Now we have real goals to achieve big success."

"Each department," PanRoo adds, "has a matrix of quantitative indicators to evaluate the performance. We also have adopted financial incentives to ensure optimal results."

"That's absurd!" Mr. B.V. squeals with a red face. "I don't know much about the words you just said. But can't you see the Virus skulking? I can!"

"Calm down, buddy," says LeDrun to his frustrated partner. "Cultivation cannot skip steps. Let's go back to the Law of Repulsion. Can anyone tell me why you're all in your Fear Bubbles?"

Silence.

"I'm afraid," woofs BarKockalotte, giving a quick look to his masters, "that I cannot find a cheaper but better third-party customer service platform in time. I could be fired!"

"I'm afraid," meows Purrplexy, licking her mouth nervously, "that with our low marketing budget, I cannot boost our market share and sales. I'm thinking about updating my resume."

"I'm afraid," says PanRoo, "we have set an unrealistic profit goal. We have a fat chance of failing with it. And Polisco does not accept failure."

"You're damn right!" Polisco growls. "We're a team of winners! We'll make the money at all costs!"

"So," Mr. B.V. reminds the polar bear, "why are you in your Fear Bubble again?"

Polisco exhales deeply like a deflated balloon. "It's the freaking engineers. Those arrogant ducks think they know everything. They won't listen! I cannot control them. I'm so pissed that I could pluck a few and have roast duck."

"I am afraid because everybody is unhappy," says Joecub, curling up in his Fear Bubble.

"I see," says LeDrun. "The Fear Bubble repels everything around it. The stress you feel comes not only from your striving to achieve a goal, but also from repelling one another. The Bubbles push each other and cause more friction. Worse, you are all in a big Collective Fear Bubble with the company's name on it."

"Look over there!" says Mr. B.V., pointing his claw at another Fear Bubble that floats toward them.

"Watch out! Enemy approaching!" Polisco roars.

10

The Slippery Slope

THE ANIMALS GAZE out through the semi-transparent membrane-like Fear Bubble. Another Bubble floats on the lake. A giant logo and company name illuminate the other Bubble's surface. On a pole sticking out of the Bubble, a purple flag waves in the wind. As the leader of his company, Polisco feels immense economic threat.

"PanRoo," says Polisco to his partner, "check out that company immediately. I want to know everything about it."

"Done," says PanRoo, staring at her computer screen. "It is a public company that makes robot workers with super intelligence. According to the latest report, their market value is 19 trillion. We are at 27. However, their growth rate is five times faster than our company's. That is to say, it will surpass us very soon."

"Let's grow ten times faster!" Polisco roars as he pounds

the conference table with his giant bear fist. "Nobody can beat us! We are the greatest of all time!"

"How?" asks PanRoo, pouring cold water on Polisco's steaming head. "We are already overworked and exhausted."

"I don't care!" says Polisco. "It's just numbers. How hard could that be?"

"Are they hiring?" meows Purrplexy, aspiring to the purple waving flag.

"Why don't you go and ask them yourself, traitor?" BarKockalotte barks, scuffing the cat and threatening to throw her out of the Collective Fear Bubble.

"Quiet!" LeDrun shouts at the quarrelsome animals. "What does 27 trillion mean to you?"

The adult animals are silent.

"Math!" says Joecub, the showy schooler.

"It means recognized value," says PanRoo, contemplating. "The public recognizes us as more valuable than the rival company. And I love public recognition."

"I love popularity," says Purrplexy hanging from BarKockalotte's paw. "Currently, we're more popular than that company, but not for long."

"I love a higher rank," says BarKockalotte, placing the cat on the desk. "27 trillion ranks higher than 19. It simply means we are better."

"What about you, Polisco?" Mr. B.V. asks the agitated polar bear. "You are the leader of the company."

Polisco takes a deep breath. "I love to win," the company leader claims. "We cannot lose this economic competition. Nobody respects losers. We must be the No. 1 economic power!"

"Win good, lose bad!" says Joecub, echoing his father.

"Do you all agree?" Mr. B.V. asks around.

"Yes!" the rest of the animals answer with loud confidence. "We love economic power!"

Under the water, a thin crack appears on the bottom of the Collective Fear Bubble. A red monster swooshes in like lightning along the crack, illuminating the Bubble with a Viral red glow. Slowly, the Fear Bubble's membrane-like surface hardens into red tampered glass. It starts to sink.

"I see," says LeDrun with a sigh. "Love does not judge. Fear does. *Power judges measurements,* thus it lords Fear Energy. *To Love Power* is the slippery slope from the Nature's Sphere toward the Viral Reality, which is fabricated by the Social Virus to disguise Fear as Love, Repulsion as Attraction, and Viral as Natural. By Nature, you all have intrinsic ability to tell Love from Fear because they use Energy—the Universal Language to communicate. The Virus has to use something *artificial* (numbers, words, concepts, symbols, constructs, etc.) to *replace* what is *natural* (value, force, message, change, quality, interconnectedness, etc.) so that you are deprived of your Naturally Rich aptitudes for perceiving, understanding, and interacting with Energy. *When it disguises Fear as Love and successfully tricks you, the Social Virus finds its way in.* Once it is inside the mind, the parasitic monster can indoctrinate the victims with what everything means and how to judge and make decisions."

LeDrun looks outside the Bubble, and then glances back inside. The animals remain inside each of their own Fear Bubbles, divided yet united in the bigger Collective Fear Bubble. He breaks out the purple crystal flask from inside his shell and takes a sip.

"How do you plan to win the economic competition?" Mr. B.V. asks Polisco.

"By growing our company ten times faster!" Polisco answers with determination.

"How?" Mr. B.V. asks with curiosity. "By giving it ten times as much water or chicken manure?"

"That would drown the company," says PanRoo.

"Or suffocate it to death," woofs BarKockalotte, backing up his master Pan.

"The company is not a damn tree, all right?" says Polisco, irritated.

"But if you want to *grow* the company," LeDrun chimes in the conversation, air quoting Polisco's words, "you must respect Nature and her Natural growth rhythm. Suppose your company is an apple tree—your unique entrepreneurial idea is like the seed. When you drop it in the right environment, it will sprout. Given enough water, sunlight, and nutrition, the seedling grows into a sapling. It blooms. The beauty attracts many. It produces apples and shares with many more. The consumers transform the Energy conserved in the fruit into their own being and carry on its Legacy. The seeds may be dropped in the right environment and grow into more apple trees someday."

"What are you talking about?" asks Purrplexy. "Bird droppings? I hate feathered animals!"

"Me too!" Joecub agrees.

"Growth," says LeDrun, ignoring the noise, "whether it be about a tree, an animal, a company, or an economy, cannot go against the Natural rhythm. You cannot push a seedling to yield overnight, or Joecub to be an adult tomorrow, or your company to grow ten times faster in a day, or the economy to rise forever. If you push hard, you will do more harm than good as you disrespect their Natural rhythm. The Law of Repulsion, remember? And you do not want to disrespect Nature. Her backfire could wipe out an entire civilization."

"Senseless," Polisco brushes LeDrun off. "Our company has nothing to do with Nature. We produce cheerleader robots, not apples! For me, right now, it is all about numbers. Nobody can surpass us if we grow much, much faster. Fruck everyone!"

"But think about where the word *growth* originates from," Mr. B.V. enlightens the polar bear.

LeDrun shakes his head and tells his teaching partner: "Let them. Notice their Fear Bubbles are firming up and getting red? That means they repel cultivation. It looks like we will have to go down with them."

As the two Messengers cross their arms and stand by, the company animals are in a business meeting. Polisco gazes at the numbers on the whiteboard for a while and then turns his head to look at his rival company. The fluffy leader takes a deep breath and delivers his speech: "My teammates, we are faced with a big challenge. Our rival company is rising at an uncontrollable speed. As industry leaders, we cannot let that happen. Our goal is to increase our market value much faster to remain in the captain's seat. I want us to unite closely to form an unyielding frontline and use your most powerful weapons! I'm going to get more funding from Hiporno and other venture capitalists. What are your strategies?"

"I don't know," says PanRoo, shaking her head. "Those are hard numbers to achieve."

"Numbers are tools," says Polisco. "You are the boss. I'm sure you can find a way to make them look prettier."

"I guess I can tweak a couple of things," says PanRoo reluctantly.

"Bark-A-Lot," Polisco turns to the dog, "what is your genius idea?"

"Master Pol," BarKockalotte grins, wagging his tail, "I can polish our customer reviews online and make them all five stars. Don't ask me how to do it. The ends justify the means. Arf! Arf!"

"Foolish," meows Purrplexy, "all foolish ideas. Who says that we cannot sabotage the enemy? Make them slow down. We get faster automatically. Theory of relativity."

The rest of the animals are intrigued.

"The media is our best friend," Purrplexy continues. "In a couple of hours, you will see reports on our rival company's scandals—dictatorial leaders, sweatshops, animal rights issues, corruption, juicy sex scandals with graphic videos, and so on. They don't have to be true. The public doesn't care about the truth. As long as they *feel* they don't like that company, we win. If one of these things happens to hold some truth, we score a touchdown."

"Wow! You're hired!" Polisco praises Purrplexy. "Let's do it!"

"The enemy is gone!" Joecub shouts out loud, pointing outside.

The confused animals look out through their Fear Bubble. They see nothing but dark, deep water. It turns out that the Bubble has completely submerged under water. Meanwhile, they notice the Bubble shimmering a lifeless red glow, like fresh blood losing its oxygen. They touch the

Bubble membrane. It is as hard as iron. The scared animals seek help from the Messengers, who just cross their arms and stand by. Suddenly, a red beam shines in through a crack in the bottom. The Bubble plummets like a freefalling elevator to the bottomless lake. The frightened animals scream and close their eyes. As if a century had passed, the Fear Bubble finally wrecks in front of a red glass palace. Above the front gate, three golden words are engraved on a red plank: House of Power.

11

House of Power

THE FAMILY STANDS in front of a magnificent glass palace. The palace is bright red, illuminating the otherwise dark world underwater. Sharply dressed political animals pass in and out of a security gate using advanced AI facial recognition technology. Polisco stares at the red glass palace. A dark feeling pulls his heart toward a painful place buried deeply in his memory. BarKockalotte howls, digging out the polar bear's trauma.

"It is the Loong King Palace!" howls BarKockalotte. "I can recognize this building despite the name change!"

"Loong King Palace?" asks PanRoo in shock. "Isn't that the headquarters of the Virus in Polisco's Inner Dimension? I thought we destroyed it!"

"I know," says Purrplexy with a pouty face. "No King, no Prince. No romance for Lexy. It sucks."

"My dad is King!" Joecub claims proudly. "I'm Prince!"

"This is NOT the Loong King Palace!" Polisco roars with flaring anger. "Are you all blind? This place is the

House of Power! LeDrun! Why are we here? My Virus is long gone. We crushed it all together, remember? So, what is this? A sick joke to torture me? You old sadist!"

"I've got this," says Mr. B.V. to LeDrun before he responds to the angry bear. The poetic beaver then offers his rhymed wisdom:

old Virus dies hard
all it takes is one little shard
the polar bear stands on a slippery slope
mistaken money for champion and hope
the Social Virus smells Fear
it promises you economic power in Viral Reality
not in Nature's Sphere
the Fear Bubble opens a crack
the Virus is in
and the Love Balloon will never come back

"What crack?" Polisco yells at the beaver poet. "I have no crack. I am perfect!"

"Calm down," says LeDrun with a smile. "Get in line. We're going inside the House."

"You calm down!" Polisco yells at the smiley tortoise. "I've seen the Virus. I can recognize that monster with its red spiky head. There is no King anymore to manipulate Power, nor Warrior here to annihilate the Prince, i.e., himself. I'm immune to all the monster's tricks!"

"Stop yelling," says LeDrun to the angry bear. "Smile at the security camera right here. Your chubby face will get us in."

"That's ridiculous," says Polisco, looking into the

camera. "I've never been here, nor am I in their stupid security system. How could they recognize my face?"

The security gate opens.

THE HOUSE OF Power is empty and yet full. It is empty because nobody is around. All the sharply dressed animals come in and become invisible like ghosts. It is full because the east wall is full of laws and regulations, the west wall history and stories, the north wall numbers and charts, and the south wall names and titles. A red, velvety chair with the golden letter "P" on the backrest occupies the center of the floor. The chair is empty and inviting. Like a nail sensing a magnet, Polisco cannot help but walk toward the chair.

"Where are you going?" asks PanRoo, pulling Polisco's sleeve to stop him.

"Didn't you see?" asks Polisco. "It is my chair. It has my initial on it."

"You mean *P*?" Mr. B.V. questions the polar bear. "It could stand for many things."

"Poop or pee, for instance," PanRoo teases Polisco.

"Or Purrplexy," meows the cat. "It could be my chair. Red is my favorite color—the color of arousal."

"It is my chair!" Polisco roars at everybody.

As the loud animals argue, a thunder-like Voice resounds in the House of Power.

"Welcome back!" says the Voice. "I missed you! Take a seat in the Power Chair, anyone?"

"Power?" BarKockalotte barks at the Voice. "Is that what P stands for?"

"Yes," says the Voice. "I've always liked you, doggie. The Power Chair is for winners. Who would like to take a seat?"

"Me! Me! Me!"

Among all the company animals, Polisco and Joecub are the loudest.

"Very well," says the Voice. "Like father, like son. Polisco, why don't you go first? Your son will follow in your steps."

Without hesitation, Polisco sits in the Power Chair, tall and proud, like a formidable warrior wearing tempered-glass armor.

"Close your eyes," says the Voice. "Think of a number you need to boost the economy of your company and, more important, to beat your rivals. The Power Chair will make it happen."

Polisco shuts his eyes tightly. He uses all his strength to push a number out of his mind.

"Open your eyes," says the Voice. "You did it. You just pumped 27 trillion F money into your company, which doubled its market value. It also beat all the rivals and became the biggest economic power on planet F. Congratulations!"

"Really?" Polisco questions. "But I don't feel anything. Are you sure we are the biggest economic power?"

"We are," PanRoo confirms. "I just checked the latest market report."

"But I don't feel anything," Polisco repeats. "I feel no joy. Nobody sings along. No resonance. No waves. No ocean. This is not how triumph and success are supposed to feel."

"I don't know," says PanRoo with a shrug. "Numbers do not lie. You may not feel the excitement because it happened too fast. When we show the numbers to the world and receive their recognition, I promise you will feel like a successful bear."

"But I feel empty," says Polisco. "Numbers are empty. I am empty!"

"My son!" The Voice sounds offended. "Look at where you sit. Numbers are numbers. When they marry Power, like the **F** money, they represent Value. As long as everyone acknowledges this social contract, it is Reality. It doesn't matter whether you feel it or not. Pursue Power, and the Power Chair will conjure up everything you want."

"By Reality," Polisco mumbles, "you mean Viral Reality."

"All right," says the angry Voice. "Your time is up. Joecub, my grandson! Do you want to sit in the Power Chair?"

"Yes!" Joecub answers with exhilaration. He runs toward the red velvet chair and shouts at Polisco: "Dad, get off the Chair. It is my turn!"

Polisco reluctantly leaves the Chair. As he descends, he turns back to gaze at the Chair, then at the whole House of Power.

Joecub sits in the Power Chair.

"What do you want, my grandson?" asks the Voice.

"I want to go up all the time!" Joecub answers.

"Ok," says the Voice. "Close your eyes and think about candlesticks."

"It's the seesaw game!" Joecub tells the Voice.

"Shh," says the Voice, "the Power Chair knows."

Joecub closes his eyes with a puzzled face. Like a toy, his body begins to inflate. Two horns squeeze out of his forehead. His fluffy bear paws harden into hooves. His fur becomes shorter and darker. His eyes pop, and his nostrils flare. The bear cub becomes a charging bull.

"What happened to my son?" PanRoo screams at the Voice in the empty House as she rushes toward her cub, only to get kicked to the floor by the charging bull.

"Hey!" Polisco roars. He asks the pets to check PanRoo while he tries to get the bull in the Power Chair under control.

The two Messengers stand by, take out their crystal flasks, and cheer for the apparent atrophy. After a couple of sips, LeDrun levitates above the Power Chair and chants:

Natural growth, Viral inflation
Natural growth is cogrowth
Viral inflation is chain-destruction
cogrowth creates an ever-generative sphere
Viral inflation incurs an unsustainable bubble
cogrowth sprouts from bonded Love Balloons
Viral inflation projects a booming illusion
bonded Love Balloons enrich each other
inflated Fear Bubbles exhaust precious Energy
Natural growth follows the Law of Attraction
Viral inflation pursues Power and incurs
the Law of Repulsion

"Mom! Dad!" Joecub's faint cry enters the loud House of Power, where the animals fight and tortoise chants.

"Quiet!" PanRoo shouts. "Did anybody else hear Joecub crying? Where is he?"

The animals look around the House. There is only a charging bull, not even a shadow of the bear cub.

A triumphant laugh resounds throughout the House. It is the Voice.

"Where is he?" Polisco roars at the laughter.

"Where he wants to be," says the Voice.

"Follow me," says Mr. B.V. "I think I know where he is."

12
Return to Natural Growth

T HE ANIMALS FOLLOW Mr. B.V.'s lead and file out of the House of Power. They turn left onto Institution Avenue with red flags on the left and blue billboards on the right, then pass the Artificial Art Museum and the Mall, take a slight right turn, and arrive at a white building. Like House of Power, it has a security gate using advanced AI facial recognition technology. Mr. B.V. signals Polisco to open the gate with his face.

"Wait a minute," says Polisco, scanning up and down at the building. "I know this place."

"Me too!" howls BarKockalotte next to his master. "It is the national treasure reserve!"

"With a golden dungeon inside it," meows Purrplexy. "But my Prince is long gone."

"Where is my baby?" PanRoo asks anxiously.

Mr. B.V. winks at PanRoo. "We'll see."

"Hey! No winking!" Polisco warns the beaver, then smiles at the security camera.

The gate opens.

The animals enter the national treasure reserve. Contrary to their memories, there are no golden buildings, silver roads, diamond vehicles, or robots made of precious stones. It is an empty house with two walls that render a real-time ticker tape matrix of rolling numbers that relentlessly go up. One wall's numbers are in red, the other in green, as if the red traffic light and the green one lit up simultaneously.

"What happened to this place?" Polisco asks, looking around. "Where is the treasure?"

"On the wall," Mr. B.V. answers, chinning up toward the walls of numbers.

"But they are numbers," woofs BarKockalotte, confusedly tilting his dog head.

"They represent treasure, allegedly," says Mr. B.V., air quoting the word *represent*.

"Right," Purrplexy mocks, "as if the Loong Prince preferred stupid numbers over gold and silver. Give me a break."

"And there is nothing to represent here!" says PanRoo with a frown. "Anyway, I couldn't care less about what happened to the treasure reserve. Where is my baby cub?"

"Master Pan," BarKockalotte whimpers, "I have a bad feeling. Since Jo is not here, there is a fat chance that he is in the dungeon."

"Let's go!" PanRoo urges. "Where is the door? Where is the window? They must have remodeled the treasure reserve!"

As PanRoo frantically searches for the dungeon's

entrance, a small window opens among the red rolling numbers. A tortoise's head sticks out.

"Long time no see," says LeDrun with a grin.

"Bulbous Head!" Polisco greets graciously. "How did you get in there? Let us in!"

A round door opens among the green rolling numbers. Like a black hole, it sucks in all the animals.

THE ANIMALS WALK downstairs. The dungeon is dark and damp, with a chilly breeze coming from nowhere. Joecub is chained to the ceiling, upside down. At the sight of his parents, the dangling bear cub starts crying like a watering can.

"Mom! Dad!" Joecub weeps. "I feel sick! I'm gonna throw up!"

"I'll get you down," growls Polisco, reaching for the ceiling.

"No!" Joecub wiggles to resist.

"What?" Polisco shouts at his son. "Why the hell not?"

"Because I'm up!" Joecub shouts back with a red face. "I'm up all the time!"

"Dude," woofs BarKockalotte, "you're not up. You're upside down."

"YOU are upside down!" Joecub cries out, fighting against the urge to throw up. "You're ALL upside down!"

"But how are you feeling, Honeycub?" PanRoo asks with concern.

Joecub vomits. "Sick," he admits.

"Eww!" Purrplexy gags out a hairball. "He makes me hurl! Do something!"

Polisco unchains the cub and places him on the floor.

"How are you feeling now, Poop Child?" the caring father asks.

"Much better," Joecub sobs. "But up is good, down bad, right?"

"Well," Polisco sighs, "trust how you feel at this moment because what you believe is not always true."

The two Messengers exchange fulfilling looks.

LeDrun levitates between the bear father and son. "Up and down are the two ends of the seesaw," he says. "One doesn't exist without the other, like waves in the ocean. When they rise to a crest, they will go down toward a trough. The circle follows the Natural rhythm. Like your breath: after you inhale enough air, you must exhale. This is also the Natural rhythm. By Nature, no waves rise forever without fall, and nobody hoards air in their lungs."

"If this is all you have for the cultivation program," BarKockalotte whines, "even Purrplexy could pass. It is a little too self-evident."

"Relax, puppy," says Mr. B.V. with a wink. "You must keep Nature in mind to find and fight the Virus. *Rich is a Natural growth experience* during which your Love Balloon bonds with many other Love Balloons to resonate, reflect, cocreate, and mutually enrich. Take your company as an example. Your entrepreneurial idea engenders from your Essence. It is unique. You send a signal—an invitation or offer that carries your Essential Message to the universe. Whoever receives your signal and resonates with the embedded Message portend toward a Love Bond with you, nearby or somewhere in the universe. When bonding, you will feel the resonance. You work together, cocreate the product, reflect each other's Essence, and enrich each other's experience."

"That's why it is called a company," says PanRoo in contemplation.

Mr. B.V., turns to Polisco. "Your Love Bonds, in case you haven't noticed, are all present at this moment."

Polisco comes to a realization. He looks at each animal. No words. Mixed feelings. The polar bear ponders in silence.

"That doesn't explain why my cub was chained to the ceiling upside down," PanRoo says while wiping vomit off of Joecub's fur.

"Patience, Pan," says LeDrun with a smile. "It is not the child. It is the adults who keep him in their Fear Bubbles and construct the Viral Reality. Some adults influence the young through cocreation, others through inflection."

"I know!" BarKockalotte howls, raising his paw like a smart student. "Viral Reality—an artificial construct designed to stimulate one's Fear constantly."

"Hold on a second," says Polisco. "The slippery slope happened when we switched our focus from cocreating the best product to making money. I was not ashamed of doing so, but I knew that was when the Love Balloon descended into a Fear Bubble on the lake. Then you two nagging noggins squeezed in. Is money the Virus?"

"Not quite," says LeDrun. "The Essence of economic exchange does not concern money. Think about a battery or a cloud that charges before a lightning strike. Like the negotiation between the cloud and the ground, it is a mutually agreed-upon quantity of Energy representing the Value of what the two parties exchange. The thunder afterward signals the satisfaction of the economic transaction to the rest of the world. The numerical monetary measurement is an artificial invention to quantify the Value of what is exchanged. It is a number, a mark, an observation of Value, but not Value itself."

"When you measure," Mr. B.V. adds, "you reach the end of Love. And when you record measurements, you reach the end of experience and the beginning of knowledge, like drawing a mark on the moving boat where the sword has dropped. Rich, if you remember, is a Natural growth experience. So, when you use money to measure experience, you stop experiencing."

"We get that," says PanRoo, like a child being told that Santa is not real. "So, is money part of the Viral Reality?"

"Not quite," says LeDrun. "Not all artificial measurements are Viral, but the Virus does use artificiality to build its colony. To craft a slippery slope from Nature's Sphere into the Viral Reality, the Social Virus has to invite Power to the show."

"How does the monster do that?" BarKockalotte barks, wide-eyed and alert.

"First, *separation*," says LeDrun. "By Nature, Essence and its observation, or Identity, are one, like wave and particle, message and signal, voidness and form, Value and exchange. The intelligent animals on planet **F** invented numerical measurements to quantify and record what you observe. Kudos for that as a Fear expert. It contributes to the **F** civilization but also makes it susceptible to a Fear-Energy-sucking monster: the Social Virus. The first thing the Virus needs to do is to *separate* the measurements from the Essence of what they observe, i.e., Essenceless measurements."

"Essenceless measurements?" PanRoo asks with a confused look.

"Yes," Mr. B.V. annotates LeDrun's words. "Essence has a tapestry of frequencies that make it unique. And the frequencies are intrinsic and ready to resonate with the world for a Natural growth experience. That is why you were BORN RICH. Essenceless measurements have been stripped away from the frequencies by the Virus. Thus, they are artificial, abstract, and unexperienceable."

"You mean data? Or math?" PanRoo feels uncomfortable as a current employer and a former teacher. "But we use it at work and teach it in school."

"The **F** animals seldom question what is used at work," says Mr. B.V., "or taught in school."

"I hate math," Polisco grunts.

"I hate school!" Joecub echoes his parents.

"Second, *replacement*," LeDrun continues the enlightenment. "Taking advantage of the separation, the Social Virus inculcates more artificial economic inventions to allegedly *represent*, but actually *replace* Essence of the measured such as money, credit, loan, interest, salary, income, insurance, stock, tax, GDP, debt. Take the economy and animals' financial lives on planet **F** as examples. Money has replaced Value; credit replaced trust; revenue replaced resonance; increase replaced growth; transactions replaced connections; stocks replaced sharing; insurance replaced caring. Essenceless measurements in artificial economic constructs have replaced the Essential experience of bonding through Love and have become the building blocks of the Viral Reality—an artificial construct where everything is perfectly calculatable, but unexperienceable. Once separated and replaced, the Virus successfully settles in the victim's mind for further indoctrination and exploitation."

"That's right," says Polisco. "Money used to represent and preserve the Value of the commodities. But **F** money is not backed by commodities, not anymore, thanks to our genius leaders. And yet we treat it as if it were," the polar bear mocks.

PanRoo raises her eyebrow. "Let's not and say we did. Is that why everyone has money on planet **F**, but nobody makes Essential things anymore? We are hollowing out."

"Essence is an ever-moving boat," says Mr. B.V. with a wink, "guided by Love, escorted by Fear, powered by Energy, and manifested by its observer. In a word, Essence is the unique experience of the Self cocreated with Others. The measurement of Essence is a momentary observation like the mark when the sword is dropped in the river. Essenceless measurement is the mark of the sword with no sword to back up the mark. In Viral Reality, the sword is a Legend, and the mark tells the story."

"Third, *Power*," LeDrun continues the illumination. "The Virus then invites Power to accelerate the slippery slope into the Viral Reality. Power is the judgment of measurements—large or small, fast or slow, strong or weak, good or bad, win or lose. The primary role of Viral Power is to reorient its subjects by telling them where they should focus their Energy—Fear Energy, of course, because Love neither measures nor judges. Power will direct the victims to make their best judgments not based on Essential experience, but on Essenceless measurements in various aspects of their lives. At this point, the Social Virus has finished building its Power center to lord its victims."

"That explains the House of Power and that damn Chair," Polisco sighs, regretting his fall into the trap.

"You are obsessed with winning the economic competition," PanRoo says, rubbing salt into the wound.

"Win is good, lose is bad!" Joecub explains his dad to his mom.

"I see!" BarKockalotte barks. "The **F** money is not backed up by commodities, but instead by the **F** government! Money and Power!"

"I happen to love both," meows Purrplexy, putting a headset on to block the barks.

"There you go," says Mr. B.V. with a shrug. "The monster's ultimate trick is to disguise Fear as Love. I won't spoil it because LeDrun speaks the **F** language better than I do. I'm a Love expert, and Love is beyond words."

"Last, *pursuit of Power*," says LeDrun with a wink. "This is how the Social Virus keeps its victims in the Viral Reality till death do them part. In Nature's Sphere, after Fear finishes protecting them from survival risks so that they feel safe again, it gives way to Love for bonding and growth. In Viral Reality, the Social Virus conditions its victims to judge Essenceless measurements and make life decisions based on *Viral preferences* disguised as Love—the more the better, the bigger the better, the faster the better, the pursuit of winning, the pursuit of owning, the pursuit of accumulation, the pursuit of popularity! From separation to the pursuit of Power, Essenceless measurements to

Viral preferences, that is how you LEARN POOR. *Rich is a Natural growth experience; Poor is a Virus conditioned mindset.*"

"BORN RICH LEARN POOR," says Mr. B.V. with his signature smile. "Self-cultivation is to be aware of the slippery slopes into Viral Reality, able to stop and return to Nature."

"I don't pursue winning," Polisco announces.

The other animals, including Joecub, point and laugh at the polar bear.

"You don't believe me?" says Polisco with a deep sigh. "Fine. I'll show it to you. Now that we saved Joecub, let us go back to the House of Power. I want to confront that Voice. I know it is the Virus."

"It's all here, my friend," says LeDrun, pointing to his head with his claw.

"I knew it!" Polisco growls at the tortoise. "Your Bulbous Head is full of Virus!"

Polisco snatches the levitating tortoise from midair. LeDrun swiftly retracts his head back into his shell and shouts from inside:

"The Virus is in YOUR MIND! Not mine!"

"What should I do? I love my head!"

"*Unlearn,*" says Mr. B.V., holding the tortoise to his chest. "Unlearn everything the Virus has infiltrated within your mind. Return to Rich."

"How? I don't know how to unlearn things."

"The Virus cannot live without your Energy. Close your eyes. Cut off the supply."

POLISCO IS IN a trance in the school principal's office. His eyeballs dart around behind the closed curtains of his eyelids while he is sitting at the desk with a stress ball in his right paw. The principal is confused and concerned. Joecub attempts to wake his dad from his trance by poking his highly sensitive muffin top.

"Dad! Dad! Wake up! Wake up!"

"I'm sorry, what?" Polisco opens his eyes with a reoriented look.

"I said," says the principal with relief, "your bear cub fought with a bull calf. Allegedly, your son wanted to have the upper paw in the seesaw game."

"I see," Polisco shakes and then nods.

"Can I go out and play with my bull friend now?" Joecub asks impatiently.

"He won't play with you for a while," says the principal. "He hurt his butt when you pushed him onto the ground. You can leave now, but you may want to apologize to your friend, Joecub."

Polisco stands up. He raises his paw with the stress ball and gently places it back on the principal's desk.

"Thank you, principal," says Polisco. "Jo, I'll play with you."

Polisco and Joecub walk out of the office. Nobody says a word. The father bear walks to the seesaw, and the son climbs onto the other end.

"Push me up, Dad!" Joecub shouts with excitement.

"You are up because of me," says Polisco. "Thank me for that."

"Thank you, Dad," Joecub pouts.

"Now my turn," says Polisco, lifting his butt.

Having no choice, Joecub falls.

"So, I am up because of you," says Polisco. "Thank you, Jo."

Joecub smiles.

"Do you see yourself up when I'm up?" Polisco asks. "Because I see myself up when you're up because of me. Self and Others are interconnected. In fact, everything is interconnected."

Joecub shakes his head with confusion. "No. I don't see it."

"Close your eyes. You will see," Polisco advises.

"I see the mind monster, Daddy," Joecub mumbles. His eyes closed, the scared child holds the purple crystal flask tightly.

13

PanRoo's Dream

THE FALL HAS arrived. The early-morning dew emits a brisk fragrance that permeates the air of Star Valley. Nature uses the softest brush to paint some leaves in saturated yellow and some in blazing red, among other stubborn green ones. This morning, she is especially busy coloring a giant maple tree in the animal family's backyard. With a heavy gust of wind, a red leaf breaks free from a twig and swirls down, landing on a meditating tortoise's head.

"Message received," LeDrun tells Nature, with eyes closed, leaving the leaf on his head like a red palmy hat.

In the master bedroom, PanRoo wakes up from a bad dream. Through her half-open eyes she sees a red leaf falling from the maple tree in the backyard. With a soft sigh, the panda kangaroo rolls over to her bear partner's side and buries her head in his fluffy chest.

"I had a bad dream," PanRoo murmurs.

"No bad, no good," Polisco mumbles in half sleep,

holding her head tightly into his chest to turn her voice into vibration. "All judgments are mutually entailing pairs of opposites. The point is—can you see good in bad and bad good? Win in lose and lose win? Big in small and small big? Hard in soft and soft hard? Hard?"

The polar bear sniggers as his new wisdom meets an old joke.

"I was the only red leaf among all the green ones on the tree," PanRoo says of her dream. "The green leaves turned into laughing hyenas. I somehow jumped off the cliff. I think my SAD is triggered by the fall."

Polisco turns his back against her and sticks his fluffy bear butt out. The butt then wiggles toward PanRoo.

"Consult your symptoms with Dr. Phinkster," Polisco introduces his doctor.

PanRoo sets foot in the doctor's office.

"Hey!" Polisco protests. "Get your foot out of my ass!"

PanRoo sighs.

Polisco snores.

"Polisco!" PanRoo yells at her inconsiderate partner.

"What!" Polisco snarls. "Let me sleep!"

PanRoo is quiet. She sends her paw to crawl up along Polisco's thigh. It arrives next door to Dr. Phinkster's office. She grabs the doorknob.

"That is the right way to wake me," Polisco moans with pleasure. "Envy, baby, envy."

"For the record," says PanRoo, pausing the motion, "I don't fancy dangling an aesthetically challenging unit under my beautiful pouch anymore. It is the Power it represents that I used to aspire to. But not anymore, because the *pursuit of Power* is the slippery slope toward Viral Reality."

"Whatever you say," says Polisco. "Just don't pause your paw."

"Self-Love is the key," PanRoo continues. "The two Messengers told us about the slippery slopes into the Viral Reality. I agree. Rich has nothing to do with having lots of money, especially the Essenceless **F** money. It is about Loving the Self. In the past, I have spent too much Energy on Others. From now on, I will pay more attention to my precious Self."

Polisco finally wakes up. "Self and Others," he exclaims. "The chicken or the egg? Self-Love sounds great if you know the Self and know how to Love. The Self is both our Essence and Identity reflected through Others. I suspect that we cannot possibly know the Self without Others, and vice versa. Same thing applies to Love. Love is the Essential Force of Attraction that takes two parties to generate. We cannot possibly Love the Self without Others, and vice versa."

"Since when did you become a wiseass?" PanRoo teases Polisco.

"On the seesaw," says Polisco with sincerity. "The other day on the playground when I played on the seesaw with Jo, I was somehow enlightened. I could see the Self in Others and Others in the Self. Do you still remember the contaminated Life Lab where the two Messengers made us look into a jar to watch how we lived and died?"

"Of course. How did you die?" PanRoo asks.

"In a war," says Polisco with a deep frown, "a trade war I started, and then turned into a nuclear war. Mine and the rivals' bodies splattered in the air and evaporated. The Death Messenger could not find my Essence."

PanRoo opens her eyes wide. "That is horrific!"

"You know what is more horrific?" says Polisco. "Our cub splattered with me. The Death Messenger could not find his Essence either. So, the other day when I was on the seesaw with him, I thought to myself that if I could see the Self in Others and Others in the Self, maybe I wouldn't wage the war in the first place. Maybe I could change how I die, and more significantly, how I live. Maybe I could share my Legacy rather than spread the Virus to the next generation. How about you? What did you see in the jar?"

"Drowning," PanRoo says in a near whisper and then immediately changes the topic. "Speaking of Power, have you heard? Sir Hippono is running for mayor of Star Valley. Rich and powerful, the cliche courtship. But the silver lining is that Pilferine is his campaign manager. I was wondering if she still has time for the HOA. If not …"

"Eww!" says Polisco, pushing away PanRoo's paw. "Why do you have to mention her in bed?"

Before PanRoo can explain herself, their doorbell rings.

"I got it!" BarKockalotte howls from the hallway.

The guard dog opens the front door.

"It's Ms. Pilferine!" BarKockalotte barks.

PILFERINE SITS DOWN on the couch in the family's living room. Due to the unpleasant past with her, LeDrun meditates under the maple tree in the backyard. BarKockalotte and Joecub play frisbee next to the tortoise. Purrplexy hides in her cat castle in the sunroom. And

Polisco refuses to get out of bed. PanRoo has no choice but to entertain this unwelcome raccoon neighbor.

"I have excellent news for you," says Pilferine with a bright smile.

"Really," PanRoo questions.

"We all know that Sir Hippono is running for mayor of Star Valley. As his campaign manager, I have so much to do to ensure that he wins. Oh! Where would he end up without me? Anyway, as a result, I have to resign from our HOA committee. What a pity! I can already see them struggling. But! I have recommended you to the committee. With Mr. Thorn's death and my resignation, you are the perfect candidate! They already said yes. The seat is yours if you want it."

PanRoo cannot believe her ears. She has been pursuing the seat on the HOA committee for so long, and yet it drops in her paws from heaven when she least expects it. Tears well up in her eyes.

"Dear Pilferine," says PanRoo to her predecessor, "you're such an angel! You won't regret it! If you ever need anything, you know where I live. Hahaha!"

"Hahah! True!" Pilferine joins the social banter. "I'd better go."

Pilferine walks toward the front door. She holds the doorknob and turns around.

"You know," Pilferine smiles, "I'm sure you will make a wise choice with your vote for mayor. Think about the HOA and your company."

AFTER SCHOOL, PanRoo and Joecub sit in the principal's office. The bear cub wears a bandage around his head.

"I am sorry for what happened to his classmate," says PanRoo. "But my son is also wounded. The school should take responsibility, don't you think?"

"Ms. PanRoo," says the principal, "you're an experienced teacher in our school. I think highly of you. However, for this particular incident, Joecub is not innocent."

PanRoo finds an excuse for her son. "He must have emulated bad peer influence at school," she says.

"Children are susceptible to many influences—peers, media, school, and most important, parents. You know that well, Ms. PanRoo. We'll give him a week's suspension this time. And hopefully, there is no next time."

"Yay!" Joecub celebrates the punishment.

"No, no!" PanRoo shakes her head. "He cannot miss school. We opt for community work."

"Haha!" the principal laughs. "No offense, Ms. PanRoo. But based on your record, community work is not your strong suit. How would you provide that opportunity to your child?"

PanRoo's face grows red. "I'm officially on our HOA committee!" she says, her voice raised. "I will create a community program for him! You watch!"

"Can I just take a suspension?" asks Joecub with a pout.

"No!" PanRoo growls at her cub. "Let's go!"

ON THE WAY home, Joecub gazes at PanRoo with angry eyes. PanRoo tries to comfort the wounded cub.

"How's your head, Honeycub?"

"What do you think? I got pecked by an eagle!"

"Did you read the book?"

"I did, every night! I just wanted to play with her."

"But why did she peck you if you wanted to be friends?"

"In the beginning I was very friendly, but soon she mocked my ears."

"What's wrong with your ears?"

"I don't want to talk about it."

"Okay. What does she look like? She is pretty, isn't she?"

"She is. But she is bald."

"Honeycub, she is a bald eagle."

14

F Names

PANROO TAKES HER wounded cub home. The rest of the animals hang out in the sunroom-turned-conference room. Polisco stands in front of the whiteboard, designing the product of his dreams. BarKockalotte sits at the conference table reading the autobiography of a barking top dog in the security industry. Purrplexy curls up on a chair, watching a documentary about a meowing guru in digital marketing. LeDrun meditates at the center of the table. PanRoo and Joecub walk in.

"Jo!" BarKockalotte woofs with deep concern. "What happened to your head? It is HUGE!"

"I got pecked by a bird." Joecub has tears in his eyes.

"Not just a regular bird," says PanRoo, placing the cub in a chair at the table. "She is a bald eagle."

"You got beat up by a girl?" Polisco heartlessly mocks his son.

"I don't know what you're implying, master Pol,"

meows Purrplexy, turning off the video. "Girls kick ass, or peck head in Jo's case."

"What exactly happened, my friend?" BarKockalotte asks Joecub.

"The other day," says Joecub, "our teacher introduced a new student to the class. Everybody laughed when the teacher said she was a bald eagle. But I thought she was the most beautiful thing I had ever seen. She sat right in front of me. I wanted to talk to her but didn't know what to say. So, I told Mom. She gave me a book about bald eagles to read. I read it and fell asleep with it every night. This morning, I decorated my white hat with white feathers before school. I thought she would like it because she had white feathers on her head too. I finally had something great to talk about with her. I said, 'Do you know why you are called a bald eagle even though you have feathers on your head?' She looked a little annoyed and asked me to call her Em. I said, 'My name is Joecub and I'm a polar bear.' She glanced at my feather hat and said, 'Do you know why you are a polar bear even though you have brown ears?' THAT upset me."

"You have your mom's ears," says Polisco.

"I know," says Joecub, giving his mom a blaming look.

"Jo," woofs BarKockalotte, "the word *bald*, according to the dictionary, has a historical meaning of *white*. Maybe *bald eagle* means white or white-headed eagle. And since you are white, technically, you could call yourself a bald bear if you want."

"I am not a bald bear!" Joecub shouts at the dog. "Anyway, after the mean remarks on my ears, she turned back around and stopped talking to me. Then I saw something hidden among her head feathers, so I plucked a feather off her head. But she got angry and pecked me!"

"You tried to pluck an eagle?" Polisco raises his eyebrow and withholds a laugh.

"Not so smart," meows Purrplexy, showing off her claws. "See those sharp claws? An eagle's claws are twice as powerful as mine."

"Your manicured claws are useless," BarKockalotte laughs at Purrplexy. "An eagle's claws are called talons. They are a hundred times more powerful than your kitty claws, and they could kill."

"Mine could kill too!" Purrplexy air scratches the dog.

"It is your fault," says Joecub to PanRoo, pouting and frowning. "I just wanted to play with Em, but you made me read a book about bald eagles. And why is she called Em and bald eagle? And why me Joecub and polar bear?"

"F names, buddy, F names," woofs BarKockalotte, teaching on behalf of his master. "They are social identities of the F animals. We all have many F names besides our real ones. Take me as an example. My name is BarKockalotte, emphasis on the *K*, thank you. But I also have many other F names—dog, pet, black, asexual, director of customer service, security officer, etc. Master Pan, for another instance, has even more F names—woman, wife, mother, teacher, yellow, immigrant, business owner, panda bear or kangaroo per her choice."

"Why?" Joecub is more confused.

"I don't know why," BarKockalotte admits. "I think our real names are uniquely ours, but the F names are shared by groups. Let's say you are Joecub. That's you, and you only. But there are millions of polar bears on this planet, so you share the **F** name with them. For those who don't know Joecub but know a lot about polar bears, the **F** name helps them identify you before they know you. Or help you know yourself. I think that's why master Pan made you read the book about bald eagles."

"Look what happened!" Joecub points to his bandaged head. "The book didn't work! And polar bears are supposed to have white ears, not colored ones."

Joecub starts weeping.

PanRoo has been quiet for a while. She ponders on Joecub's reaction to his yellowish-brown ears, the ears that take after her. The bear cub seems to have a Fear Bubble about those ears.

"Honeycub," says PanRoo to Joecub, "why were you upset at Em?"

Joecub glances at PanRoo and lowers his head.

"She made fun of my ears," Joecub mumbles.

"Is that why you wear a white hat to school lately?" PanRoo asks her son. "It is NOT because it gets chilly in the morning, is it?"

"They're not white," Joecub admits, lowering his head. "They're yellowish-brown panda ears. They call me Panda Ears at school!"

Now Joecub starts bawling.

PanRoo takes a deep breath.

Polisco frowns without words.

Purrplexy immerses herself in grooming.

BarKockalotte uses his book to poke the meditating tortoise's shell.

"LeDrun," the dog whimpers, "say something wise, please!"

LeDrun opens his eyes and stretches his arms. He then stands up on the table, paces back and forth, and chants:

Essence and Identity
the Self via Others
Essence is nameless; Identity forms names
Essence is unique; Identity is mutual
Essence is continuous; Identity is contextual
through Love, the Force of Attraction
Others resonate with Essence and form Identity
the Self is a co-creation experience with Others
through Fear, the Force of Repulsion
the Self pushes Others away to
protect the Essence and
maintain the boundary of Identity
Love Balloons
bond with each other
to form an interdependent community
in which Essence enriches the Self and Others
Fear Bubbles
define the field of the Self from Others
in which Essence is safe from invasion
Collective Fear Bubbles

...

"What is wrong with panda ears!" PanRoo yells at Joecub.

Her furious voice startles the chanting tortoise. He shuts up and retracts his head inside the shell.

"They are not white!" Joecub cries. "I want white polar bear ears like Dad's!"

"As long as you can hear," says the enlightened father to his son, "your ears are fine."

At last Joecub reveals the real reason. "But they laugh at me!"

PanRoo suddenly hears thousands of hyenas laughing. She takes a deep breath and tries to calm down. She recalls the bed talk about Self-Love this morning. After quite a while, she says to Joecub in a peaceful tone: "You are a unique bear, Sweetcub. You were endowed with different magics from the Origin, the big ball, remember? Your ears are the evidence, and you should be proud of them. The entire community will see how special you are."

PANROO FINISHES HER first HOA meeting. Her proposal to build a community program for children is approved by the committee. She comes home and gathers the whole company in the conference room. The panda kangaroo sits at the conference table, as ravishing as a blooming tree on a bright spring day.

"Guys!" says PanRoo with excitement. "The HOA committee approved my proposal. We'll host a carnival for the children in our neighborhood. Neighbors will get acquainted with each other, and Joecub will make new friends! First, we need to go door-to-door to send invitations and collect their real names as well as their **F** names."

"Objection," Polisco growls. "I have serious safety concerns about us going door to door in our neighborhood. Given how friendly our neighbors are, we have a fat chance of being shot due to trespassing."

"Or a mass shooting at the carnival," Purrplexy chatters with flattened ears. "I refuse to go to any public gatherings nowadays, not to mention hosting one."

"I would avoid Mr. Thorn's house at all costs," BarKockalotte whimpers. "His ex-con second son lives there now."

PanRoo's face turns gloomy, then resentful. She glares at Polisco and growls in a trembling voice: "As a husband, you're supposed to have my back whenever I need you. And the carnival is not even for me. It is for your son!"

"Wait, what?" Polisco feels attacked from ten different directions. Before he can defend himself, PanRoo turns her weapon toward BarKockalotte.

"Mr. Bar," says PanRoo in tears. "As a dog, what is your best virtue?"

BarKockalotte lowers his head. "Loyalty."

"Then show it to me," says PanRoo. She aims her gun at the cat.

Purrplexy immediately waves the white flag. "Do whatever you want," she purrs. "I'm just an employee."

"Good," says PanRoo, color returning to her face. "Let's continue. I've divided the neighborhood into four perfect districts. Joecub and I will collect the statistics of the east district. Polisco …"

"Will Em be at the carnival?" Joecub asks in anticipation.

"No, Honeycub." PanRoo smiles at her son and explains the community program. "The carnival is for our neighbors living in this community. You can make new friends!"

"No! I want to play with Em! It is all your fault!"

The bear cub throws another world-class temper tantrum.

The animals all look at PanRoo.

PanRoo whispers to the tortoise shell: "LeDrun, please do something. Remember how I revived you in my pouch?"

LeDrun reluctantly sticks his head out. He lies on the tabletop. His green and purple chest button pops up.

"Paws on my chest," LeDrun shouts toward Joecub's direction. "Let's go back to the I Resort for another Love Balloon ride."

"Balloon ride?" Joecub stops crying. "Wait for me!"

15
Communal Company

THE ANIMALS OPEN their eyes in the lobby of the I Resort. Tents and booths of various sizes and colors occupy the place. Campers hold different signs and shout out their righteous causes. Volunteers hand out pamphlets at the booths and introduce their lofty missions that help many other underrepresented groups. All the shops are closed. Security and police animals are nowhere to be found. Broken windows of the shops are like wide open mouths screaming silently in the darkness. Advertising signs and billboards are overpainted with names, logos, and graffiti of animal external reproductive organs. Spats and brawls ignite like confetti poppers and fireworks, celebrating the most splendid animal civilization.

"This place stinks!" Purrplexy meows. "It smells like a thousand dogs."

"Hey!" BarKockalotte barks. "Leave the canine population alone."

"Fight for! Fight!" Joecub is stimulated by the scene in the lobby.

Polisco shushes Jo. "Shh! What is this place? I thought the I Resort was full of skyscrapers and construction sites. What is this circus about?"

PanRoo takes a deep breath. "I find it fascinating," she says.

"LeDrun," woofs BarKockalotte, "is this the same I Resort we visited last time? How come it looks completely different?"

"Because the Love-disguised-Fear is different this time," LeDrun smiles, motioning toward PanRoo with his chin. "PanRoo's Fear is not Polisco's Fear. Thus, the Social Virus fed by her Fear Energy renders a different world of Love-disguised-Fear around her. Follow me. Watch your feet. Don't step in any number one puddles or number two mines."

The Death Messenger levitates and leads the way. The rest of the animals follow him on their tiptoes. Finally, they make it to the elevators, only to discover that they have been gentrified into mobile shelters for needy animals. The family greets the residents and gets stared at during the brief encounter. Finally, they arrive at the Love Terrace.

THE LOVE TERRACE is just as crowded, but less feisty. A digital kiosk equipped with a virtual queuing system stands tall and upright. A long line of animals quietly awaits numbers to be taken. Those who have their numbers sit on the marble floor in anticipation. Some carefully review their application documents, ensuring all of the forms and supporting documents are there. Some close their eyes and quietly rehearse their answers for the upcoming interviews. Others stick their necks out and gaze from the Terrace to admire numerous giant balloons floating in the air. They all have cubic gondolas that hang below. The square LED screens on the gondolas proudly exhibit diverse group names, official identities, social titles, cultural tags, and so forth. The scene very much reminds PanRoo of her **F** card application process. Among the waiting-to-be-picked animals, a beaming beaver waves at them with both paws and full dentures.

"Over here!" Mr. B.V. shouts and beckons.

The animals come over to join Mr. B.V. at the outer corner of the brisé-fan-shaped Love Terrace.

"Guys," says Mr. B.V., "what is the emergency? I was summoned in quite an urgent manner. You know this is the Love Terrace for your Love Balloon trips. There is one thing you cannot rush or push in your life, and that is Love. If you push Love, you'll end up on its flip side. We all know what that is."

"Mr. B.V.," Joecub explains, "I don't like my panda ears, but my mom doesn't like that I don't like my ears."

Mr. B.V. laughs with affection. "Haha! You know I am deeply fond of juggling, words included. Nice feather hat by the way!"

Mr. B.V. pats Joecub's white feather hat.

Joecub's face wrinkles up as if he smells something rancid.

"Ahem-kum!" Polisco interjects with a fake cough.

"Juggling aside, since we are here, should I take us on my Love Balloon trip? The dream office is waiting for us."

"No upside down!" Joecub shouts, recalling the trauma of being chained to the ceiling last time.

"What about PanRoo?" LeDrun asks. "Do you still remember your Love Balloon trip?"

"How can I forget?" says PanRoo with sparks in her eyes. "It is my dreamland—a bamboo forest, a creek with plenty of fish, a hunting crane, galloping horses, and roaming sheep on a grassland."

"Does it sound good to you?" Mr. B.V. asks Joecub.

"Yes!" the bear cub applauds.

"Pan," says LeDrun, "to attract your Love Balloon, you want to send out an Essential Message for a Love Bond. The Love Balloon must receive it and resonate with it. That is how the Law of Attraction works. Last time when we were here, Polisco failed to attract his Love Balloon because he wanted to attract money, yet money as a medium did not have Essence. In other words, money didn't have a frequency of the Self to form resonance with Others."

"Not a problem for me," PanRoo says with confidence. "Polisco doesn't know what he wants. I do. I have dreamed about that place so many times. I can close my eyes and take us there in no time if you all could stop talking."

"Hey!" Polisco protests. "As a newly enlightened bear, I'm offended."

"Be offended quietly," says PanRoo to her partner. "I'm concentrating on attracting my Love Balloon. Hold my paws, everyone. I'll take you to the place of my dreams."

The animals sit down in a circle, holding paws. PanRoo closes her eyes. A smile emerges on her face. It is a joyful smile that springs from the bottom of her heart. Meanwhile, a leaf-shaped, sage-green Love Balloon floats toward the Terrace.

PANROO'S DREAMLAND IS as dreamy as it was during the last visit. The bamboo forest is still emerald and soothing. It sings a country duet together with the gentle breeze to greet the distinguished guests. The white crane spreads her wings in the sunlight by a clearwater creek. Fish swim above the colorful pebbles of the creek bottom. Marshmallow clouds in the sapphire sky cast fluffy shadows on the velvet grassland, where bay horses are galloping, and black nose sheep are roaming. Before PanRoo introduces her dreamland, the rest of the animals all fly away like birds freed from a cage. Polisco jumps into the creek to catch some big fish. Purrplexy disappears into the bamboo forest to search for a castle. BarKockalotte joins the bay horses and runs wild with a big tongue-hanging smile. And Joecub rolls around in the grass among the black nose sheep. PanRoo feels a strong wave inside. Tears come out.

"Are you crying?" Mr. B.V. asks.

"Joyful tears," PanRoo answers.

"Congratulations," says LeDrun. "You have formed instantaneous Love Bonds with everything and everyone in here, thus a Natural community. You are all from Nature. And all Nature's children speak the same language—the Universal Language beyond words. The wave you feel is the resonance between the unique frequency of your Essential Message and the bonding frequency of theirs. When a

Love Bond is formed, you receive tremendous Energy from Others and resonate with larger waves. You become bigger than your Self. It is Rich—a Natural growth experience."

"Could we gather everyone here?" says PanRoo as tears continue to fall. "I want to build our company into a true Love-bonded community."

EVERYONE IS PASSIONATE about PanRoo's vision of the Love-bonded company community. It has a park, a cafe, a library, an art gallery, and a recreational center. The creek is its natural aquarium, the bamboo forest its botanical garden. Polisco insists on having an outdoor cooking area so that they can grill fresh fish caught in the creek, or just chill out with a beer after work. The excited animals work together to build their community. Mr. B.V. chews down enough sturdy bamboo for the cabin. LeDrun takes care of the beaver's teeth like a good dentist. He offers the purple elixir from one crystal flask to the beaver to swish and spit, and then the green elixir to sip and swallow. Two horses, Gal and Nay, volunteer to carry all the materials to the construction site. Polisco and BarKockalotte build. Purrplexy decorates. A black nose sheep, Gloom, affectionately weaves the finest wool into the plushiest carpets. On the celebratory day of the completion of the company community, the crane, Hook, brings drinks carried by his strong wings and several stringers of fresh fish hung from his beak. Mr. B.V. offers to grill the fish. LeDrun holds a timer to help the questionable chef. Polisco starts a fire pit on the deck. Joecub shows his new horse and sheep friends how to toast marshmallows. PanRoo sits in a rocker by the fire with a purring Purrplexy on her thighs. Mr. B.V. brings a plate of burnt fish and joins the animals.

"This is the ultimate Rich life to me," says PanRoo with a joyful smile. "The dreamland, dream company and all of you—Love and being Loved.

"Me too," Polisco agrees. "We probably could use better grilled fish."

The beaver chef makes a face and flips the polar bear some burnt fish.

Immersed in all the joy and laughter, PanRoo watches the dancing bonfire flames and listens to the crackling charcoal music. Suddenly, an idea creeps into her mind.

"Sweetcub," says PanRoo to her joyous child, "do you want to know your new friends' **F** names?"

"I love my new friends," Joecub smiles.

"I'm sure you do," says PanRoo. "But our company is a community that embraces diversity. When you recognize and embrace their **F** names— species, age, gender, sextual orientation, ethnicity, colors of fur, etc., you will show to the world how loving and inclusive you are. There is a whole knowledge base available for young minds like you to learn. Let's move to our brand-new library for lesson one on **F** names—color differences."

16
Self and Others

PANROO REGATHERS THE animals in the library. Outside the windows, the bamboo forest starts to wither. The grassland slowly turns earthy brown. The creek dries out, and the exposed pebbles on the bottom decompose. Shadows of dead bamboo leaves break in through the bay window and settle on the books, whiteboards, a tireless presenter, and a yawning audience.

"The color of fur," PanRoo lectures with a book in her paw, "is a fundamental category of **F** names for social identification and demography."

"What's demo-graphy?" Joecub asks with innocent eyes.

"Great question!" PanRoo praises the youngest student in the class. "Anybody know the answer?"

"I know!" BarKockalotte raises his paw like a start student.

PanRoo skips the canine go-getter and picks the feline daydreamer.

"Purrplexy, do you know the answer?"

"What's the question?" Purrplexy meows as she lays her head on the table and uses her paw as a pillow.

"Define demography!" BarKockalotte barks at the absent-minded student.

"Never heard of that," Purrplexy yawns. "But I have an extensive acquaintance with P-O-R-N-O-graphy, so my best guess is abovesaid with a demo?"

The adult students in the class crack up. The youngsters cluelessly follow.

"Mr. Bar!" PanRoo raises her voice to maintain classroom order. "Could you please tell the class what demography is?"

"Absolutely!" BarKockalotte howls like a champion. "Demography is a statistical study of animal populations. It is a proven key to learning and regulating animals through grouping variables."

"Excellent!" PanRoo praises wholeheartedly. "Most **F** names can be found in demography. To know the Self and Others, those names provide important information. And to build our Love-bonded company community, they play an indispensable role. We want to include animals with the widest variety of **F** names."

"Bor-i-n-g!" Purrplexy yawns out her opinion.

"I don't want to study!" Joecub shouts and pouts. "I want to play!"

"Honeycub," says PanRoo patiently, "don't you like the white feather hat? The **F** names are like colorful hats. See your dad? What color is he?"

"White," Joecub answers.

"That's correct!" PanRoo encourages. "What about Mr. Bar?"

"He is a little black, grey, maybe brown, a little white …" Joecub tries to differentiate all colors of the dog's fur.

"His **F** name is black," PanRoo explains. "How about your new friends?"

The horses neigh. The sheep meh.

"Gal and Nay are brown. Gloom is black-and-white."

"Brown is right. Gloom shares the same **F** name with Mr. Bar."

"What color are you, Mom?"

"I'm … um … yellow."

"You're not yellow. You're white, black, and light brown!"

"My **F** name is yellow. There are only five **F** names for the colors of fur."

"Who decided the colors?" asks Joecub. "I don't think they are very smart. You see, Mr. Bar is smart, but Purrplexy is not."

"Hey!" Purrplexy protests.

"Oh, they were very smart," says PanRoo with a smile. "They just made it simple so animals like Purrplexy can follow."

"Seriously?" the offended cat hisses.

"Listen," says PanRoo, "the whole point is that no matter what color you are assigned to, you should be proud. Joecub, you should be proud of your yellowish-brown ears because they make you special. In addition, you want to Love other colors as well because we are a community."

"How come Joecub's color is special, not mine?" meows Purrplexy. "My fur used to be white, but after the incident at Pilferine's, you know, my fur now has a greyish hue. I think I'll invent a new **F** color called Lexy Grey."

"If grey meant i-grey-nance," BarKockalotte mocks. "Historically, they only invented five colors for **F** names. You cannot change that."

"They?" Purrplexy hisses. "Who's they? Why should I care?"

Polisco frowns. "Are you sure about including the **F** names in our company? Because I have a very different understanding of what a Love-bonded community means."

Joecub is completely confused. "I already Love my new friends," he says. "Do I have to know their colors? If I do, do I Love them or their colors? What about myself?"

PanRoo struggles to answer the questions.

While PanRoo's teaching is being challenged, the library transforms into a large, semi-transparent Bubble that is stationed near a lake in a desert oasis. The bamboo forest disappears. Dry, thorny bushes take over. The grassland recedes. Endless sand dunes dominate. The crane, the bay horses, and the black nose sheep fade away. Through the thorny bushes, many pairs of red, watchful eyes blink in the dusk. PanRoo's dreamland turns into a spooky desert. The Love Balloon gives way to the Fear Bubble.

EACH ANIMAL IS enveloped in their own Fear Bubble inside a much larger Collective Fear Bubble. They shout, argue, and fling verbal poo bombs at one another. The two Messengers stand by, sip their drinks, and watch the cozy family show.

Joecub finally notices the change. "My friends are gone!"

The adults shut their mouths and check around.

"Where are we?" asks PanRoo, checking outside in shock. "This is not my dreamland! It is a desert!"

"Wait a minute," says Polisco in sudden realization. "I can recognize the lake and the bushes. This is where I met you in the **D** Lair last time, right Pansycakes? You were in disguise among a group of laughing hyenas."

"I disguise myself when I'm in Fear," says PanRoo as she reflects. "Camouflage is my weapon. But I'm not in Fear now. How in the hell did we end up in a Fear Bubble in a desert? LeDrun, Mr. B.V., you two did something fishy backstage, didn't you? Care to explain?"

"Not me," says Mr. B.V., waving a burnt fish in his paw. "Grilling was the only fishy thing I did."

"Me neither," says LeDrun with a shrug. "It was the Law of Repulsion. When you opened up and shared your dreams with other animals, your Energy dynamics with them followed the Law of Attraction. When you identified them with **F** names without bonding with their Essence, you reached the end of Love and the beginning of Fear. That was how the Law of Repulsion took over. By the way, welcome to my big **D** Lair!"

"Nonsense!" PanRoo roars. "The whole idea of the community program was to teach Joecub about Self-Love. You know he is self-conscious of the color of his ears. That's why I started with the color of fur in the library. And for your information, on planet **F**, **F** names are the most common way for the animals to know the Self and Others—school and job applications, patient forms, TV and cyber space, political elections, social events, neighborhood scuttlebutts, you name it. Children learn about them both formally and informally. So, what is wrong with me educating my child?"

"It is not about right or wrong," says Mr. B.V., putting a charred fish into his mouth. "It is about Love and Fear." The Life Messenger then renders his rhymed poem:

the cub got pecked by a bald eagle in school
the mother thought hosting a carnival would be cool
her dreamland attracted dream friends
they built a Love-bonded company community
colors did not matter, faces or their rear ends
the party turned into a lecture
F names, colors surely matter
Others in Bubbles, Self in Fear
Law of Repulsion, shifted into gear

PanRoo gets angry. "What Self in Fear? I just said I am NOT in Fear! And what Others in Bubbles did you mean? The hyenas? Because I don't see them anywhere!"

"No Others, no Self," says LeDrun, taking a sip from his purple crystal flask. "The Self is your ID—I the Essence, D the Identity. Essence is your core. Identity is your boundary. Together, they form a unique, ongoing, and interactive experience with Others. Others are the contextual, interactive, and reflective participants that reflect your Identity and/or observe your Essence. When Others become your Essential Observers, Self-Love and Others-Love become one. The F names, however, are complicated. First ..."

"Fear Bubbles invasion!" BarKockalotte barks urgently to warn the family and shut down the illuminating tortoise.

The panicked animals rush to the semi-transparent boundary of their Collective Fear Bubble and investigate the situation. Numerous Fear Bubbles of different colors have besieged them. On the surfaces of the Bubbles, they loudly display their names, logos, and the causes that they righteously fight for. As the Fear Bubbles get closer and closer, the animals discern armed bay horses, armored black nose sheep, and, unsurprisingly, the cackle of hyenas.

17
Frames of Reference

THE FAMILY IS besieged by numerous Fear Bubbles. Nobody knows where they originate and how they emerge. Inside some Bubbles, they recognize the hyenas, bay horses, and black nose sheep. Many other Bubbles, however, are less apparent as they seem to include all kinds. The family must read the names, logos, and tags on the surface of the Bubbles. PanRoo starts panicking. She pleads to the two Messengers.

"Please, do something!" says PanRoo.

"Why?" LeDrun asks, sipping from his purple crystal flask.

"Why?!" PanRoo shouts. "Look at them! They are so close!"

Mr. B.V. winks at PanRoo. "I thought you wanted to be inclusive."

"But did you hear the hyenas?" PanRoo yells at the unsympathetic beaver. "They are laughing!"

"I want to play with my friends!" Joecub cries as he sees his new friends in the Fear Bubbles nearby.

Mr. B.V. whispers into LeDrun's ear. The Death Messenger sighs and says, "Let's take a cruise. It will buy us some time, but not long."

The tortoise raises his arm and points to the lake like a captain. Following his command, their Collective Fear Bubble bounces up into the lake and buoys up and down with the waves. PanRoo feels relieved as she sees the increasing distance between them and other Bubbles that dwindle into dots back in the direction of the desert lakeshore.

"Much better," BarKockalotte howls. "A safe distance is necessary."

"What was that about?" Polisco asks, referring to the Fear Bubbles flooding in. "It happened so fast! Where did they all come from?"

"I bet they live here," meows Purrplexy. "LeDrun's **D** Lair is a creepy haunted place."

"Here?" woofs BarKockalotte. "Maybe the hyenas, but the horses and sheep belong to master Pan's dreamland. I couldn't fathom why they appeared in the **D** Lair. Are they following us somehow?"

"Bingo," says LeDrun. "They followed PanRoo's mind. She wanted to build a community-oriented company that includes animal employees with all sorts of **F** names. Here they are."

PanRoo rolls her eyes at the tortoise. "Thank you for telling me what's on my mind," she says. "It didn't add up. I wanted to build an inclusive community brimming with

Love, not filled with Fear. Where did all the Fear Bubbles come from?"

"Argh, the stubborn mind," Mr. B.V. says, frustrated. "Love does not call names. It bonds, cocreates, and mutually identifies. The **F** names you prescribed to them are out of Fear, or worse, the Virus."

"Nonsense!" PanRoo insists, raising her voice. "We all need names. Otherwise, what do we call each other? Hi and hey?"

"Don't argue for the sake of arguing, PanRoo," LeDrun admonishes. "We all know what kind of names we are discussing. They are not individual names, but group names that the **F** society assigns to you. Identities are temporary and contextual. Once the interaction is over, the Identities dissolve. Holding on to the names of Identities reaches the end of experience and the beginning of knowledge. Essenceless names deprive Nature's children of their uniqueness."

"I know we are all unique," says PanRoo, holding Joecub in her arms. "That's what I'm trying to teach to Jo. But the **F** names are widely used references that the cub must understand."

LeDrun shakes his head, feeling exhausted. "The Frames of Reference," he says. "When you were born from the Origin, there was no distinction between the Self and Others. They were one. As your Love and Fear, the two Essential Forces, interact with other forces in the world, you gradually develop an understanding of the Self in relation to Others. Guided by Love, you bond with Others to see your Essence through their reflection and generate your Identity via mutual recognition. Guarded by Fear, you draw boundaries against Others to protect your Essence and reinforce your Identity. *The ongoing experience of your Essence and Identity together with Others is what you refer to as the Self.* As for Others, in a Love Bond, they are your Essential Observers. In a Fear Bubble, they are your Frames of Reference."

"I know the frame of reference!" BarKockalotte howls proudly. "I got an A in physics at the Canine Police Academy! It is a measuring system for moving activities. Some frames of reference have observers that relate to the observed. The observers are sometimes in motion but pretend they are not."

Purrplexy leers at the pedantic dog. "Your mouth is in motion, but I pretend it is not."

"Quiet!" LeDrun disciplines the pets and then turns to PanRoo. "You cannot observe Others without the participation of the Self. In the physical world, frames of reference measure moving phenomena. In your mind, Frames of Reference measure Others as well as the Self. The fallacy many **F** animals commit is that you thought the Self was an independent observer from Others. That was why you used **F** names on Others but attempted to teach Joecub about his uniqueness. The Self is a participant observer of Others. The Self-Other relationship is always mutually reflective."

"That is to say," Mr. B.V. adds, "when you put Others into a color Bubble, you simultaneously put the Self into a color Bubble. You did say you were yellow, didn't you?"

"What if," BarKockalotte woofs, putting his tail between his legs, "we end up in the same Bubble with, let's say, the hyenas?"

"Eww," Purrplexy gags with disgust. "I will never be in

a Bubble with hyenas because we don't share any similar-ities. BarKockalotte, however, looks a lot like a hyena."

"Fun facts," BarKockalotte smirks, "hyenas are much closer relatives to felines than canines. So, Love your cousins, Lexy. They are family."

"A Collective Fear Bubble," LeDrun explains, ignoring the sparring pets, "is when you use a much bigger, much more inclusive Fear Bubble to encapsulate the smaller Fear Bubbles. Look around. You are each in your own Fear Bubble and on top of that, you are all within a Collective Fear Bubble together. When you are in a Collective Fear Bubble, the members use the same Frames of Reference to conform with one another and ensure the shared similarities that identify the group. Individual Fear Bubbles inside the Collective one inflict Law of Repulsion against each other to cause heat for social volatility and violence. Collectively, they must have common enemies to justify the coerced conformity. In a nutshell, a Collective Fear Bubble serves culture dishes of internal coercion and external aggression."

"So, everybody is in Fear," says Polisco, picking his nose. "Speaking of family, is that a Collective Fear Bubble, too? I thought family was a bouquet of bonded Love Balloons. What about our company? Star Valley? The planet F?"

The Death Messenger smiles and levitates. He bounces off each animal's Fear Bubble and chants:

Essence vibrates with Essence
Identity respects Identity
The Virus separates Essence from Identity
Love attracts to bond and cocreate
Fear repels to protect the boundary
the Virus replaces Love with shared boundaries

Love Balloons resonate between diverse forms
Fear Bubbles conform to collective similarities
the Virus replaces bonded Love Balloons
with Collective Fear Bubbles
Love Balloons connect Self with Others
through shared experience
to build a symbiotic community
Fear Bubbles highlight in-group similarities
and inter-group differences
and use them as Frames of References
the Virus disguises shared group names
as Natural communities
bonded Love Balloons enrich each other
for a Natural growth experience
Collective Fear Bubbles shield the members
from group Identity crises
the Virus paints Collective Fear Bubbles
as colorful Love Balloons

"So, you didn't answer my question," says Polisco with dissatisfaction.

"Master Pol," woofs BarKockalotte, wagging his tail, "I think the family could turn into a Fear Bubble sometimes. For instance, when Purrplexy threatens to quit for a new home or … or … master Pan coerces us to host the neighborhood carnival."

The dog lowers his voice and avoids eye contact with PanRoo.

"I think the company could turn into a Fear Bubble," meows Purrplexy, "when we hire animals based on their **F** names or work with a bunch of Essenceless hats."

"How about the **F** society?" Polisco ponders. "Is it a giant Collective Fear Bubble?"

"All Love Balloons could turn into Fear Bubbles," LeDrun enlightens the animals, "especially when you put Others into their Fear Bubbles first to induce the Law of Repulsion. A Collective Fear Bubble emerges when a group is invaded, and the members have a common enemy. They are still in their individual Fear Bubbles, so there is a lot of tension and conflicts among the individual Bubbles. When they fight together against the invaders, they are temporarily united but not bonded. A Collective Fear Bubble could happen to planet **F**. In fact, the Self of an individual animal could inflate into a Collective Fear Bubble if you hoard and protect all Essenceless **F** names assigned to you by society."

PanRoo rejects this angrily. "Ridiculous! Our family and our company are both Love Balloons. Say *I Love my family. I Love my community. And I Love my Self.* Say it, Jo, say it!"

While Joecub struggles to resist, under the water, a thin crack appears at the bottom of their Collective Fear Bubble. A red monster swooshes in like lightning along the crack, illuminating the Bubble with a Viral red glow. Slowly, the Fear Bubble's membrane-like surface hardens into red glass. Meanwhile, large Collective Fear Bubbles of all sorts of animals—horses, sheep, hyenas, snakes, and others emerge from under the water and besiege the family again. They encircle the animals like a pack of wolves, keeping a cautious distance.

"No!" PanRoo shouts in panic. "What's happening?"

"They are here for your Love-bonded community

company," says Mr. B.V. with his signature smile. "Will you embrace them?"

PanRoo is tongue-tied. She checks the colorful Fear Bubbles around her, then sets her eyes on Joecub. With a deep breath, PanRoo holds Joecub's little paw and says with determination: "LeDrun! Get us close to them! I'd like to greet our new friends and show my Love."

"Okay," LeDrun winks at Mr. B.V., who tightly holds onto the tortoise's shell to brace himself.

Captain Tortoise then raises his right arm and directs the Collective Fear Bubble to move ahead.

"Ahoy!" PanRoo greets them with a perfect smile as they get close to the colorful Fear Bubbles.

Graciously, all the Collective Fear Bubbles open fire at the animals.

Water streams in through the fresh bullet holes. The attacked animals plummet into the lake like little Titanics.

But the lake seems bottomless.

18
Return to Natural Resonance

B EFORE THEY DROWN in the bottomless lake, a swirling waterspout forms like an underwater tornado and swallows them up. The frightened animals eventually land on a giant rock. A torrential waterfall thunders down in front of them.

"Wait a second," says Polisco, looking around. "I know this place."

"I hate water," meows Purrplexy. "First creek, then lake, now waterfall. Can we go back to civilization, please?"

"It is the school!" BarKockalotte howls to echo Polisco. "It's master Pan's Shapeshifting School. I can see the Hippo Campus. It's right over there!"

The dog points to the two seahorse-shaped buildings in the valley.

"Impossible!" PanRoo gasps as if she just woke up from a nightmare. "The Shapeshifting School was a Viral Reality in my Inner Dimension. But we crushed it! No more social performances, no more role simulations, no more Socialicus! I am Virus free!"

"All it takes is a shard," says LeDrun with a smile. The Death Messenger crosses his legs and meditates on the big rock in front of the waterfall. "Remember the pile of red shards I asked you to decipher in the clouds? They are the ruins of the Virus's Power Centers. After it exhausts its victim's Energy, the parasitic monster escapes the dead body for new colonies and blows up its old headquarters into pieces. Those Viral ruins are invisible to your mundane eyes, but we Messengers can see them. They are everywhere."

"We could see them too!" says Polisco. "I remember that red pile in your igloo."

"Me too!" Joecub agrees. "It cut my paw!"

The cub raises his bear paw and shows everyone a scar on his palm.

"It was because you were with a Messenger," says Mr. B.V. with pride. "When you become a Messenger someday, you can see everything."

"There is a bug," woofs BarKockalotte.

"What? Where?" Purrplexy hisses with flattened ears. "I hate bugs! Can we *please* go back to civilization?"

"A bug in what LeDrun said," BarKockalotte explains to LeDrun, ignoring the ignorant cat. "You said that the Virus escapes and seeks new colonies after the old ones die. But we all beat the Virus and are still alive. Where did the shards, or the Viral ruins, go?"

"How do you know you are alive?" asks Mr. B.V., winking at the dog.

"What?" "Holy box!" "Are we dead?" "No!"

The Life Messenger's playful words cause panic and chaos among the animals.

"Mr. B.V.!" LeDrun scolds his partner. "Don't joke about their deaths to mortal animals."

"Why not?" says Mr. B.V. "It's Nature's marvelous design."

"Because they don't understand it!" says LeDrun. "Look what you did to them. They're scared!"

"Guys!" LeDrun raises his voice. "Calm down! Mr. B.V. is joking. You're not dead!"

"Not yet," Mr. B.V. mumbles.

"To address Mr. Bar's question," LeDrun continues, "yes, you adults have all beaten the Virus in your Inner Dimensions, thanks to me and Mr. B.V.'s help. You are welcome. However, the monster's Power Center ruins were left inside you. If you feed them enough Fear Energy, they will revive and re-possess your life."

"So, it's like when a recovering alcoholic slips up and has a drink," meows Purrplexy.

"Or a flare-up of an old disease," woofs BarKockalotte.

"Or a living nightmare like this," says PanRoo, looking at the Hippo Campus in disbelief.

"Fear is necessary, though," says Polisco with his new wisdom. "It is half of the equation. How do we know when it protects us and when it feeds the Virus inside us? What is the slippery slope?"

LeDrun gazes at the Hippo Campus. "Let's find out the answers together in PanRoo's mind," he says.

THE CAMPUS IS crowded. Animals wearing various hats march toward a white, neoclassical-style building. Each one of them looks like PanRoo dressed in a different style. LeDrun signals the gang to follow the marching PanRoo crowd. They pass by the Business School, Department of Women's Studies, Institute of Mother Science, the Education Lab, the Immigrantology Center, Institute of Languages and Cultures, the Wife Art District, and finally arrive at the front gate of the magnificent building. Like the House of Power, the entrance to the building is equipped with AI facial recognition technology. The family animals look at PanRoo for the key.

"Don't look at me," says PanRoo in denial. "I don't recognize this place at all!"

"Yes, you do," says LeDrun with a smile. "It is your place. Look at the camera."

"No!" PanRoo covers her panda face with both paws.

Polisco calls on the rest of the animals. "Let's help master Pan," he says. "Remember how she made us do the carnival?"

The polar bear then peels down PanRoo's paws from her panda face. BarKockalotte holds the left one, Joecub the right. While Purrplexy provides her a most relaxing paw massage on her back, Polisco affectionately holds her chin up and angles it toward the camera. A perfect smile automatically appears on PanRoo's face in front of the camera.

The gate opens.

"Welcome back, our Valedictorian!" the Voice greets PanRoo and her gang.

THE ANIMALS ENTER an auditorium. The surrounding walls are filled with names and descriptions, numbers, indexes, references, tables, charts, symbols, illustrations, maps, legends and demo videos. An empty red chair sits on the bare stage, behind which is a large screen projecting an image of PanRoo and her perfect smile. The seats are all taken. The members of the large audience look like PanRoo wearing different hats.

"What is this place?" PanRoo asks. Tremendous Fear floods her from head to toe.

"It is your Inner Dimension," Mr. B.V. beams like sunshine. "See all the stuff on the walls? Those are your cheat sheets to learn about the Self and Others."

"That's hilarious," says PanRoo with a nervous laugh. "I don't like bragging, but I need no cheat sheets when it comes to learning. I always know the answers."

LeDrun joins the conversation. "What about questioning what you learn?" he asks. "What if the school were a Shapeshifting School? What if the teachers were all Socialicus? What if your textbooks were all cheat sheets?"

PanRoo ponders.

"I use cheat sheets in school," Purrplexy admits. "That doesn't stop me from being an extraordinary cat."

"I think you're just an extra ordinary cat," BarKockalotte mocks, intentionally pausing after "extra."

"What's what I said, Dummy!" Purrplexy is annoyed.

"So, what if we cheat a little," Polisco asks, quickly adding. "I mean as learners, of course, not spouses."

"Good question," says LeDrun. "Self and Others are

one. They project onto each other. Therefore, the way you know Others is the way you know the Self because that is the only way you know how. The Frames of Reference are two-way streets."

"I don't believe a word you say," says PanRoo with a frown.

As the animals argue, a familiar Voice resounds in the auditorium.

"Ladies, gentlemen, and the above and beyond, let's welcome our Valedictorian!"

The audience throws applause, shouts, and boos toward the stage.

"Ms. PanRoo," says the Voice, "please take the Power Chair on the stage."

PanRoo looks around, flustered. "Me?"

The rest of the animals push her onto the stage like electrified pranksters.

PanRoo sits in the Power Chair.

"Now," says the Voice, "you are in Power. Use it to make your name a Legend."

PanRoo thinks for a second, then commands from the Chair: "May our company be a Love-bonded community that includes all kinds!"

The audience is quiet.

"No male polar bears in the company! Their time is up!" an audience member shouts and throws a hat at PanRoo on the stage.

"No police canine!" another hat is thrown on the stage.

"**F** male!" "**F** police!" "**F F**!" an angry uproar shakes up the auditorium.

PanRoo is panicked. She runs off stage and scolds the two Messengers.

"Look what you did!"

"Power again," says LeDrun, wiping off the growling panda kangaroo's spit from his face. "To craft a slippery slope from Nature's Sphere into the Viral Reality, the Social Virus has to invite Power to the show."

"Separation first?" BarKockalotte tilts his head as he recalls the cultivation in the House of Power last time.

"Yes," LeDrun confirms. "The first slippery slope to the Viral Reality is always *separation*, so the Virus can creep in and meddle in the middle. In PanRoo's case, it is the separation of her Essence from Identity, thus the Self from Others. In Nature's Sphere, Essence and Identity are one. Essence is unique, and so is Identity. However, intelligent animals invented **F** names based on groups. Identity is mutual, contextual, relational, interactive, and temporary, whereas **F** names are collective, fixed, prescribed, divided, and artificial. In other words, **F** names are Essenceless references."

"So, the **F** names of PanRoo," says Polisco in contemplation, "are like woman, wife, mother, teacher, business owner, yellow immigrant?"

"As long as they are devoid of her uniqueness," Mr. B.V. illuminates while juggling three hats.

"Second, *replacement*," LeDrun continues. "Taking advantage of the separation, the Social Virus inculcates more artificial social inventions to replace the Essence of the individual, such as gender roles, professional titles, relationship status, and colors of fur. Take the **F** animals' social lives for example. Professional titles have replaced social Values; relationships have replaced connections; groups have replaced communities; promotions have replaced growth; ethnicities have replaced characters; colors have replaced virtues; and so forth. It is an artificial construct where everybody is perfectly identifiable and referable. Once separated and replaced, the Virus successfully settles in the victim's mind for further indoctrination and exploitation."

"Self is an ever-moving boat," says Mr. B.V., putting all three hats on his head. "Others are the meaningful encounters along the journey. Essenceless names entail no meaningful encounters but a pawful of established marks, docks, and destinations."

"Third, *Power*," LeDrun continues. "The Virus then invites Power to accelerate the slippery slope into the Viral Reality. Power is the judgment of references—good or bad, correct or incorrect, appropriate or inappropriate, proud or ashamed, admirable or despicable. The primary role of Viral Power is to reorient its subjects by telling them where they should focus their Energy—Fear Energy, of course, because Love neither frames nor judges. Love bonds and cocreates. At this point, the Social Virus has finished building its Power Center to lord its victims."

Mr. B.V. adds his wisdom. "As you all know," he says, "the mind monster's ultimate trick is to disguise Fear as Love so that it can keep the victim in the constant Fear Loop until death gives it another jump start."

"Last, *pursuit of Power*," LeDrun continues. "In Nature's Sphere, Love and Fear flow in harmony—*Love gives way to Fear when in danger; Fear gives way to Love when safe.* In Viral Reality, the Social Virus conditions its victims to spend constant Fear Energy to live up to their **F** names, not to their Essence. It is Fear because **F** names are not about the resonance between the Self and Others. If doctors live up to their **F** name, they don't truly care for their patients; if teachers live up to their **F** name, they don't truly cultivate their students; if leaders live up to their **F** name, they don't truly have concern for the members; if parents live up to their **F** name, they don't truly nurture their children. *Rich is a Natural growth experience; Poor is a Virus conditioned mindset."*

"BORN RICH LEARN POOR," says Mr. B.V., looking at PanRoo with his signature smile. "Now we are all in PanRoo's School of Power, where she learns about the Self and Others."

PanRoo does not reply or defend herself. She takes a deep breath and goes back to the stage. Before confronting her Virus, she sees Joecub sitting in the Power Chair already. The bear cub looks around the cheat sheets on the walls. Suddenly, he spots a bald eagle in a list of symbols.

"I want to play with bald eagles!" Joecub squeals with anticipation.

A flock of giant bald eagles fly onto the stage to grant his wish. They grab Joecub with their sharp talons and swoop out of the auditorium. The family chases the birds from the campus to the waterfall, where they drop the cub into the torrential water.

"Joecub!" PanRoo jumps off the cliff without hesitation.

LeDrun sits on the large rock and shouts downward: "*Unlearn* to save the child!"

PanRoo wakes up from a nightmare. Through the bedroom window, she sees a red leaf falling from the top of the tree, like the way she fell off the cliff in the dream. Polisco mumbles to remind her that today is her day to take the cub to school. PanRoo hurries to get up and urges Joecub to have breakfast and get ready. In the car, PanRoo notices Joecub's white feather hat.

"Nice hat, Jo," says PanRoo.

"Thank you!" says Joecub excitedly. "I am going to talk to Em today! I know a whole lot of bald eagles!"

"She is a bald eagle," says PanRoo calmly, "then you are a polar bear with panda ears. She is a bird, then you are a mammal. She is a girl, then you are a boy. She is Em, then you are Joecub."

"I don't understand," Joecub frowns and subconsciously pulls his hat down to cover his ears.

"She is your mirror," PanRoo smiles, patting Joecub's feather hat. "And you are hers."

"Em doesn't have a mirror," says Joecub with sparks in his eyes. "Maybe in her backpack?"

"It is her eyes," PanRoo says. "Remember you can see two little Joecubs in Mr. B.V.'s eyes? You want to see two little Joecubs in Em's eyes, not two little polar bears who worry about the color of their ears."

"I'm not worried about my ears!" Joecub insists.

"You have a mirror in your eyes, too," PanRoo continues. "If you have bald eagles rather than two little Ems in your eyes, she may not be your friend."

Joecub is quiet for a while.

"Mommy," says the bear cub, "can I tell you a secret?"

"Sure, Honeycub," says PanRoo. "What is it?"

"I really like Em," Joecub admits with a shy smile. "But when I look into her eyes, I see something familiar. It gives me bellyache."

"It is called déjà vu," says PanRoo. "It happens, especially to someone in Love."

"No, Mommy," Joecub takes a deep breath. "I see the red monster in her eyes."

19
The New Boss

I T IS A Monday morning. The bear couple is away, having been summoned by Sir Hippono's lawyer for an urgent business meeting before sunrise. Joecub woke up crying after a twilight nightmare where the mind monster ate his brain. After patting and comforting the cub back to sleep, BarKockalotte brings the local newspaper in. He makes himself a cup of Dragon Well tea, tiptoes into the sunroom, closes the door, carefully places the hot teacup on the conference table, rolls up the newspaper into a tunnel, extends it into the cave in the cat castle where Purrplexy sleeps, releases some squeaky natural gas from his rear end reserve into the pipeline, turns around, and starts barking.

"Arf! Arf! Time for work!"

"Meowk off! The masters are not home. Let me sleep. Eww, what is that smell?"

The smirky dog takes a seat near the cat. He bites the plastic wrap off the newspaper, opens the first page, and reads the sensational headlines aloud.

"Animal Trafficking Equipped with New Technology"

"Another School Mass Shooting. Shooter at Large"

"Come on!" Purrplexy protests, half asleep. "I just had an intimate dream. Don't be a buzz kill, okay?"

"Fine," woofs BarKockalotte, putting down the newspaper and picking up the teacup. "How about Rich? I'm sure that's a topic you'd entertain. I've learned so much about it from our masters. You see, according to master Pol, Rich is not about Having lots of money because the **F** money contains neither intrinsic Value nor experiential Worth for Natural growth. And according to master Pan, Rich is not about hoarding **F** names because the **F** names contain neither individual Value nor bonding Worth for Natural growth. In my humble opinion, Rich is about *what you Have*, which determines your Love Worth. The more you Have, the Worthier you are; the Worthier you are, the more Love you receive; the more Love you receive, the Richer you become. For instance, I Have a job, a roof over my head, a bed to rest in, and some toys to play with. I also Have a family—two masters, Jo my buddy, LeDrun my mentor, and you. I must say that I am a very Rich dog."

"Bla-bla-A-lot," says Purrplexy, mocking the dog's name, "with the emphasis on bla. I'll assure you that you don't Have me, not in any way, shape, or form."

BarKockalotte thinks fast for a counterargument. "Well, you know what I mean. I Have a family. You are family. So technically speaking, I Have you."

"No, you don't!" Purrplexy is annoyed. "Nobody can Have me, not even my boyfriend. I am a free spirit! And the roof, the bed, the toys, and Joecub are not yours either. They are the masters'. You Have nothing."

"A Worthless cat wouldn't understand," the dog fights back. "By the way, you can argue that I do not Have you, but you cannot deny that our masters Have you. They can prove it with your adoption paperwork and your employment contract."

Purrplexy thinks for a while.

"Quiet. You're a bore," the cat finally meows, turning her back on the dog and pretending to sleep.

BarKockalotte contentedly takes a sip of his tea and resumes perusing his newspaper.

"Hate Crime Escalated to Species Genocide"

"Blast at Mayoral Campaign Event. Hippo Candidate Killed"

"What hippo? *The* hippo?" Purrplexy jumps out of her castle. "Read that piece to me."

BarKockalotte turns the page and finds the piece of news. After a quick read, the dog bears the tragic news:

"Sir Hippono died in a bombing at his campaign event yesterday. Pilferine—his campaign manager and romantic partner—died on the way to the hospital."

"Everybody dies," Purrplexy sighs. "Sooner on this infested planet rather than later."

"Speaking of which," BarKockalotte woofs, "how will *you* die? You know, we have all seen our destiny in a jar at the contaminated Life Lab."

"Suicide," Purrplexy mumbles. "How about you?"

"I will die a civil war hero," BarKockalotte howls.

"Hero on which side?" Purrplexy questions.

As the two pets mourn the couple's deaths and their own, the masters bring home a box of documents and a little raccoon orphan.

"Good!" Polisco says with a folder in his paw. "You two are up. Bark-A-Lot, wake Joecub up so he can meet his foster sister. Let them play in the living room. You join us in the conference room. The couple's death has caused an earthquake."

THE ADULT ANIMALS leave the dazed little bear and confused little raccoon in the living room while they have an emergency business meeting. Polisco takes out a pile of paperwork from the box and spreads it out on the conference table. Purrplexy curls up in her seat, chewing the tip of her tail and observing the new situation. PanRoo stares at the teacup, then turns to the dog. "Mr. Bar," she asks, "is this my Dragon Well tea?"

"Yes," BarKockalotte hurriedly pushes the teacup toward his master and spills the tea all over the table. "I made it for you, master Pan."

Purrplexy holds her tail and laughs out loud.

"Shh!" Polisco shushes everyone. He waves a folder in his paw.

"Sir Hippono was killed during a campaign event yesterday," says Polisco. "We were informed by his lawyer this morning that his only child, his three-year-old daughter, has become the new owner of our company."

"What does that mean?" BarKockalotte barks nervously.

"I bet nothing changes," Purrplexy meows calmly. "The three-year-old new owner can barely spell her name."

"Yet she is officially the youngest multi-billionaire in town," says PanRoo, sipping her lukewarm tea.

BarKockalotte looks upward with admiration. "What is her net **F** Worth?"

"You mean what she owns minus what she owes?" says PanRoo. "I don't know the exact number, but I guarantee you that she could buy many towns like Star Valley if she wanted. You know what's crazy? This morning when we arrived at the meeting, besides the lawyers, there were about a hundred of Sir Hippono's family members fighting for custody of his daughter. They were the most spiteful hippos I have ever met. Anyway, the meeting served as one of their qualifications to be able to run the commercial empire on behalf of the little hippo until she finishes her higher education."

"So, they took over our business?" BarKockalotte whines in distress.

"Hahah!" Polisco laughs. "They tried. You should see the looks on their faces while we were explaining the robot industry and the market for our products. It turned out that they were all consumption experts. None of them knew how to create things."

BarKockalotte reads the files on the table, feeling increasingly confused.

"According to the contract," says BarKockalotte, eyes on the paper, "the three-year-old hippo is the owner of the company, and we are the actual operators of the company. Then who do we presume to actually *Have* the company, the owner or the runners? What about her guardians who will oversee the whole commercial empire on her behalf? Will they participate in our business meetings? Will they make business decisions? But they know very little about robots. Can they fire us? I have lots of Fear about this new situation."

"Good questions," says Polisco, scratching his fluffy head. "It's called legal ownership, Bark-A-Lot. Technically, the three-year-old boss owns the company and can do all the things mentioned above, including firing us. However, I do not see any of these scenarios panning out. She is the owner on paper. We run the company for real."

"Who would Have the company then? The owner or the runners?" BarKockalotte is disturbed. "I believe that Rich is about what you Have because what you Have determines how much Love you are Worthy of by Others, i.e., the Love Worth. However, what does it mean to Have? The more I think about it, the less I understand it. Earlier, Purrplexy claimed that she was unHaveable. Now, a three-year-old and her guardians Have the company on paper. They own the company, but we run the company. Does the little hippo's net F Worth contain our Worth, or vice versa? And master Pan said the little hippo's net F Worth could buy many Star Valleys, but we are the actual residents that give the town life. Who are the Rich? Who are the Worthy?"

"I don't have answers for you," says PanRoo, pointing into the living room direction. "But we did sign the paperwork to foster our deceased raccoon neighbor's child to honor the verbal will that she left to the first responders on the way to hospital. Two orphans, two destinies. Sir Hippono's family bitterly fought over his daughter's custody whereas Pilferine's daughter had been left alone in her mom's van crying when we picked her up."

"How come?" Curious, BarKockalotte tilts his head. "I thought they were a couple."

"Dating didn't count," Purrplexy sits up to cleanse her face. "Pilferine had to marry the rich hippo to have access to his money and stuff. You wonder why marriage needs a license?"

"I bet Joecub is so happy," says BarKockalotte with a smile. "He Has a new sister!"

"Again," Purrplexy argues, "nobody can Have nobody."

BarKockalotte raises his intelligently superior brow. "Double negative?"

As the two pets banter, the new siblings fight in the living room.

"It is *my* choo-choo train!" Joecub shouts at his foster sister.

20
Whose Choo-Choo Train?

THE TWO CHILDREN sit on the floor. Joecub grasps the chimney of the choo-choo train while the little raccoon pulls hard on the caboose. Before the two kids break the toy in half, BarKockalotte, the savvy babysitter, butts in for mediation.

"Jo, could you share your toy with your raccoon sister?"

"No! It is my choo-choo train!"

"Sweetheart, could you play with something else, a raccoon Barbie, maybe?"

"No! I want the choo-choo train!"

The dilemma does not daunt the dog. He fetches a stack of receipts from the toy box.

"Jo," says BarKockalotte, handing a slip of paper to the bear cub, "give me the toy and take the receipt. You are the owner of the choo-choo train. It won't hurt your Love Worth no matter who plays with it."

Joecub hesitantly releases the toy.

"Sweetheart," BarKockalotte says to the little racoon,

"now you can play with the choo-choo train. But legally speaking, it is Joecub's toy."

"I don't care. I am Having it now!" the little raccoon grins.

"What about me?" Joecub feels bamboozled.

"You can play with the receipt!" the little raccoon suggests.

The two children get into another fight.

BarKockalotte's patience runs out. He pounces in front of the little raccoon, snatches the toy from her paws, puts it back in the toy box and with great determination locks all the toys up.

"There!" BarKockalotte barks. "Nobody gets to play with the toy if you two keep fighting!"

Joecub waves the receipt at the little raccoon. "It is my choo-choo train!"

The little girl cries. The little boy grins.

"Where is the key, Dumbass?" Purrplexy wipes the smirk off BarKockalotte's face.

The dog whimpers at the masters and wags his tail.

PanRoo shrugs. Polisco crosses his arms.

Joecub yells at BarKockalotte upon realizing that he cannot access his toys.

"I want my toys right now!"

"Here they are, buddy!" BarKockalotte hands over the whole stack of receipts to Joecub.

The little boy cries. The little girl grins.

"Why did you bring her home? It is all your fault!" Joecub blames his parents for bringing a foster sister into his life.

The deeply frustrated little bear tosses all the receipts

up in the air to cause confetti rain, then throws another world-class temper tantrum.

The little raccoon glares at her new foster brother as if she saw a red-eyed monster.

"LeDrun!" the couple shouts, seeking help from the wise tortoise.

The tortoise appears on the coffee table, smiling at his bear prodigies.

"*All you Have in life is experience,*" says LeDrun to the couple. "PanRoo and Polisco, as two newly enlightened Messengers, it is time to trust your ability to illuminate those who are lost on the journey. Let's start with your child."

"Messengers? Who?" Polisco does not believe his ears.

"Enlightened? Us?" PanRoo is too stunned to move.

"Okay," says LeDrun patiently. "Take your time to internalize."

He then levitates in mid-air and chants:

Love experiences Having
Fear protects what you Have
Love opens up possibilities to attract Others
to cocreate Worthy experiences
Fear shuts down the border against Others
to secure exclusive resources
Love initiates mutually Having experiences
between the Self and Others for cogrowth
Fear aims to secure the boundary of the Self
and gain recognition of Others
Love sends Essential Messages to the universe
and receives Energy for your Love Worth
Fear employs your Energy to safeguard

what you Have as proof of your existence
Love is Having dynamic experiences at present
Fear maintains the Had in the past
and aims to Have in the future
Rich is the Self
Having Worthy experiences with many Others
Poor …

"Ouch!" the little raccoon cries out. "Joecub hit me!"

She then pounces on the offender and scratches his bear face.

"They are *my* toys!" Joecub shouts as he defends the raccoon attack. "This is *my* home! *My* parents and pets! Everything is *mine*! Nothing is *yours*! You're a Worthless garbage scavenger!"

The orphan bawls with heartbroken tears.

"Joecub!" PanRoo growls at her son. "This is her home too. She lost her father last year and her mother yesterday. If you were her, how would you feel?"

Joecub gives his mother an angry side eye but does not say a word.

"Dude," says Polisco, teaming up with PanRoo, "how many toys do you Have in this huge box? A hundred? Do you think you can play with them all at once?"

"They are all locked inside the box anyway," Joecub cries.

Polisco reels the cub in. "I'll make you a deal," he says. "If I can open the toy box, you want to share your toys."

"Okay," Joecub agrees conditionally. "But I want the choo-choo train!"

Polisco runs to the garage and comes back with a long-handled wood splitter.

"Oh, no!" howls BarKockalotte. He protects the toy box with his body. "Master Pol, is there a less destructive way to open the box?"

Polisco rests his paws on the end of the long handle. "I don't know. Who locked the toy box again?"

BarKockalotte lowers his dog head with embarrassment. He then suddenly raises his head with a shiny grin.

"I know a place!" BarKockalotte woofs proudly. "It is a magic place with abundant toys!"

"Where is that?" the two kids ask with excitement and curiosity.

THE I RESORT in BarKockalotte's mind is well organized with educated animals. The gang arrives in the lobby, where a pawful of Love Balloon airlines booths are brightly erected. Some passengers in long lines await the AI-assisted slow self-check-in kiosks, while others in longer lines wait for the slower robots at the counters to check in their luggage. BarKockalotte struts toward Flying Bone Airlines to purchase Love Balloon tickets. The rest of the animals follow his lead.

"Good morning, Sir," says the Airline staff robot with a programmed smile. "What can I do for you?"

"Six Balloon tickets, please," BarKockalotte woofs with confidence.

"What class?" the flight robot asks.

"Umm," BarKockalotte hesitates, looking at his masters.

"No worries, Sir," says the flight robot, raising its right hand with a touch screen.

"Give me a high five," the robot waves the screen. "The system will render the best tickets for you based on your net **F** Worth."

The dog gives the robot a high five.

"Six economy tickets, Sir," the robot hands over the Love Balloon tickets.

"Wait," BarKockalotte barks at the robot. "What about business class or first class tickets? Are they available?"

The robot smiles. "They are exclusive tickets, Sir."

"What are you implying?" BarKockalotte feels disrespected.

"It is not me, Sir," says the robot. "It is the system. Have a pleasant trip!"

The gang makes their way to the elevators for the Love Terrace. Each elevator specifies the class of ticket holders it exclusively serves. While waiting for the economy elevator, BarKockalotte creeps over to the first class elevator and presses the "up" button. The offended elevator immediately reprimands the rude dog:

"Class trespassing! Class trespassing!"

21
The Dog's Love Worth

THE ELEVATOR OPENS to the brisé-fan-shaped Love Terrace, which is divided into different gateway sections by glass walls. The economy gateways section is the smallest and most crowded. The seats are all taken by jaded passengers and their dreary carry-ons. Through the glass wall they can see a luxury lounge with cafes and wine bars. Several passengers enjoy their drinks and work quietly on their computers. The two kids press their faces against the glass divider. The adult animals peel them off the glass wall and elbow their way through the crowd to arrive at their gate, where Mr. B.V. and his grandkit await.

"What is *he* doing here?" Joecub rolls his eyes at the little beaver.

"Nice to see you too!" Mr. B.V. greets the gang. "My grandson insisted on joining the Love Balloon journey with his two friends."

Joecub claims ownership of the toy. "The choo-choo train is mine!"

"Don't listen to him," says the little raccoon, holding paws with the little beaver. "Mr. Bar said there are abundant toys there."

"Yay!" The little beaver is excited.

"They are all mine!" Joecub warns the newcomers.

"Come on, guys!" BarKockalotte interrupts the young animals. "Our Love Balloon is boarding."

"I want to go there!" Joecub shouts, pointing to the first-class lounge through the glass divider. "They Have nice things!"

"That's right!" BarKockalotte howls. "Be a boy with big dreams! Someday, you will be in the first-class lounge."

The flight staff robots call the groups by number for boarding. The animals get in line, waiting for the robots to take care of the priority boarding group first.

"So," Polisco checks the long queue from head to tail, "we share your Love Balloon with all of them? So much for uniqueness."

"Well," BarKockalotte woofs, "the crater lake has been sold to a real estate developer and turned into a mixed-use district. My dream home is now in a nice community. It is true that the houses share the same design, but the insides are completely different worlds. Plus, we all have unique addresses. I proudly painted my own house number and designed the Beware of Dog sign."

"I hate cookie-cutter homes," PanRoo mumbles. "It looks like a graveyard from a bird's eye view."

"We live in one of those graveyards," Polisco reminds his bear partner.

"I know," PanRoo pouts.

"Aren't those homes all mass-produced identical twins?" Mr. B.V. asks.

"Mine is special," BarKockalotte woofs with pride. "It is the model home."

THE ANIMALS STAND in front of the bone-shaped model home. It looks exactly like all other homes except the house number. BarKockalotte lets everyone in and gives them a grand tour. In the living room, there is a wall full of TVs; a wall full of pictures of family, friends and famous dogs; and a wall of wooden logs surrounding a large fireplace. Various awards are displayed on the mantel. A painting of the happy animal family hangs above the fireplace. In the home gym, there is enough fitness equipment to train a whole city. In the library are enough books to teach an entire university. In the kitchen, food reserves could last for a century. And in the garage, cars could transport a whole army. BarKockalotte skips his bedroom and opens the door next—a toy room.

"Choo-choo trains!" the kids scream with excitement. "Can we play?"

The dog host grins affectionately. "Absolutely!"

The kids fly into the toy room like birds embracing the sky. The little bear organizes the choo-choo trains into a column formation. The little raccoon links the trains together into a super freight line. The little beaver stacks up the trains into a choo-choo tower. They play, laugh, and make choo-choo sounds. They attach a string of tennis balls to the train cars to fashion a yellow locomotive caterpillar.

They add Frisbees to both sides of the train as wings and make it fly. They compose a choo-choo song chorused with squeaky chew toys accompanied by dog bowl percussion. BarKockalotte is inspired. He joins the team with a creative idea:

"Do you want to build a choo-choo train station with food and music?"

"Yes!" The three young minds are excited.

"*Love is Having together,*" says LeDrun, smiling affectionately at the four bonded animals. "*Fear is to Have alone. Having and to Have, the experience of the Self via Others.*"

"Speaking of Having and to Have," Mr. B.V. chimes in, "Mr. Bar lives by the lake shore. The crater lake is stunningly beautiful, thanks to Nature. Anybody care for a lakeside walk?"

PanRoo raises her paw. "Count me in! Mr. Bar said the whole lake area has been developed commercially. What else are out there?"

"Yes!" BarKockalotte wags his tail among the choo-choo trains. "There are water parks, shopping centers, a business district, an art district, and tons of restaurants and bars."

Purrplexy wants to party. "Let's go out! Why are we still in your doghouse?"

BarKockalotte checks the playing children and hesitates.

"Take them with us," Polisco suggests. "Isn't your dream home a Love Balloon? Make it fly."

"Master Pol," BarKockalotte whimpers, "it used to fly, fly high. But ever since I settled here and began accumulating what I Have, it has flown increasingly lower and slower until it is now permanently stationed. I don't mind, though. I Love what I Have."

"Bore!" Purrplexy pouts. "I don't care. I'm going out with or without you."

The cat goes for her purse. The dog swiftly scuffs her neck for a freeze.

"No coercion," LeDrun scolds the dog, making him release the captured cat. "Your dream home gets heavier and heavier as you accumulate what you Have without Having the experience with Others. Having together originates from the bonding resonance between the Self and Others, thus shared Energy. However, everything you claim to Have requires your own Energy, and your own Energy alone, to maintain and protect. Since you only Have so much Energy to spend, you have less and less Energy for the Love Balloon to bond and fly. Why do you accumulate so much in life?"

"Because it is my Love Worth!" BarKockalotte explains. "When I was a puppy, everybody Loved me. Who doesn't Love a cute puppy? But as I grow up, I must go through education and then occupation—my diplomas and certificates, my awards, my relationships, my occupations as well as everything else I own. In total, they comprise my Love Worth. As you can see, after years of hard work, I am now a quite Worthy and Loveable dog."

"No, you are not," Purrplexy gives the proud dog a side eye. "You get stuck in here!"

"The Love in the Love Worth," says PanRoo, filling the awkward silence. "Is it for what you Have intrinsically or extrinsically? It seems to me that all the things you accumulate are extrinsic, like an expanded boundary of the Self for Others to recognize and respect. That is okay but that is Fear, not Love. No Love, no growth. No growth, no Rich."

"The Worth in your Love Worth," says Polisco, sniffing his stubby fingers. "How do you determine it? Or do you let Others determine it for you? Or is there a statistical formula that normalizes the conversion? Do you use the same mindset to determine other animals' Worth as well? That, my friend, goes beyond the Love realm of connection and enters the Fear realm of calculation."

BarKockalotte has tears in his eyes. He feels punished by his masters.

LeDrun cheers up the dog as well as everyone else. "Good news, Mr. Bar! You are in luck today. We have four Messengers gathered in here, who will share our Energy to help your Love Balloon fly."

"Four Messengers?" BarKockalotte looks around with sad puppy eyes. "I thought we only had two Messengers— you and Mr. B.V.. Are there two more invisible ones that secretly help you guys the whole time?"

"Brahahaha!" LeDrun laughs graciously. "Polisco and PanRoo are the newly graduated Messengers."

"Congratulations!" Mr. B.V. blossoms like a flower.

"I knew you two were special when I saw you at the adoption agency!" BarKockalotte cries with happy tears. "I am so proud of being your dog!"

Purrplexy is envious. "Why not me?" she wants to know. "I believe I am better than them because I'm the best."

Polisco still cannot believe his ears. He ponders for a while and then turns to the once again shocked PanRoo: "He said it twice. It must be true regardless. We are

Messengers now. We can finally go to the Sanctuary. And we probably will never die."

PanRoo shakes her head in disbelief. "I don't know," she says. "I don't think I am as enlightened and magical as LeDrun and Mr. B.V.. I feel like I need a much longer time to cultivate my wisdom and enlightenment."

"Enlightenment does not take time," LeDrun smiles. "It takes moments, the enlightening moments that illuminate the bonding and boundaries, the Self and Others. Once you are enlightened, the wisdom will grow because you can see the outside, the inside, and the interconnectedness between the two."

"That is how you revive Love and return to Rich," says Mr. B.V.. "And for the record, when your mortal avatars perish, you die. Others bonded with you via Love, however, will carry on your Legacy, so you live on with them. They are your new avatars."

Something important occurs to Polisco. He whispers his concerns into LeDrun's ear.

"Barhahah!" The wise tortoise is humored. He asks Polisco: "Are those things Natural?"

"Absolutely!" Polisco answers. "Everybody does it, including the president of the **F** planet!"

"Then, yes. You can still pick your nose and make fart jokes," LeDrun assures the new

Messenger.

"How about my ball—" Polisco pushes the limit.

LeDrun shakes his head. "You will find the balance with Others."

"They are perfectly balanced," Polisco mumbles.

"Wait." PanRoo has another concern. "Are we Death Messengers or Life Messengers?"

"Same difference," the two Messenger chorus.

"So," Polisco is eager to practice his chops, "how exactly do we induce our Energy into BarKockalotte's Love Balloon?"

"When you make a Love Bond with Others," LeDrun offers, "it forms a resonating phenomenon between one of your Essential frequencies and theirs sent as a Love Message. Mr. Bar, would you Love to fly high?"

"Yes!" BarKockalotte howls passionately.

"Then send the Love Message to the universe with your deepest passion," Mr. B.V. encourages. "The four Messengers will receive the Message and resonate with you. Once we bond, you can access our Energy, and that my doggy friend, is your Love Worth."

BarKockalotte closes his eyes then opens them back up. He whimpers: "I don't know what my deepest passion is."

"You're passionate about building the choo-choo train station, aren't you?" asks Mr. B.V.

"I am," BarKockalotte frowns. "But I don't know if it is the deepest. I need more data to compare and analyze before I can draw a scientific conclusion about my passion."

"We have no time for your nerdy nonsense," Purrplexy hisses. "Just close your eyes and meditate on your dreams."

BarKockalotte closes his eyes. A smile emerges on his face like a sunrise. His bone-shaped dream home rises up like a helium balloon. The sky is boundless. The lake glitters with gold and silver. A thought glimmers like a purple bolt of lightning in BarKockalotte's inspired vision.

22

The Exclusive Club

BARKOCKALOTTE'S BONE-SHAPED HOME flies over the densely populated crater lake commercial district. Through the large window in the library, the animals see all sorts of shops, restaurants, hotels, theaters, parks, and so forth. Thousands of tourists, locals, families, and couples enjoy what the lake district has to offer. As they fly over a shopping mall, Purrplexy asks to be dropped off. BarKockalotte, however, neglects the cat's demand. He seems determined to take his family and friends to the destination of aspiration. Finally, the dog's Love Balloon stops above a beautiful, quiet lake shore with nothing but luxury mansions shining up through the thick of the woods and private yachts glittering on the water.

"What is this?" Purrplexy yells at the dog. "Go back to the mall!"

"The destination of the choo-choo trains," BarKockalotte announces. "It is the exclusive club that I always want to experience, but I am not a club member. Look at the private beaches and docks. Look at the mansions. What a privilege!"

"It seems that the exclusive club takes up four-fifths of the lake resources," Polisco observes over the window. "Most animals are congregated in the one-fifth section of lakeshore."

"What is exclusive?" the little bear asks.

"Exclusive is to Have something to the Self or your group, excluding many Others," BarKockalotte explains.

"What is private?" the little raccoon asks.

"Private is to Have something to the Self or your group, not sharing with many Others," BarKockalotte explains.

"What is privilege?" the little beaver asks.

"Privilege is to Have something to the Self or your group, inaccessible to many Others," BarKockalotte explains.

The three children look at the expository dog, their confusion mounting.

"I know what a club is," Purrplexy also likes nurturing young minds.

"No, you don't!" BarKockalotte barks at the cat. He then looks at the three curious young minds and says: "Follow me to the toy room. I'll show you how things work."

The three children follow the canine teacher to the toy room. The rest of the adults stand by and watch the show. Meanwhile, the Love Balloon starts descending. All the security systems of the exclusive club properties detect the invading balloon and target it with the most lethal weapons.

IN THE TOY room, the young pupils sit on the floor while Mr. Bar piles up many toys for teaching. Then he sits down and picks up a red choo-choo train.

"Do you like playing with the choo-choo train?" BarKockalotte engages the students' learning interests like a good teacher.

"Yes!"

"Great!" BarKockalotte continues. "Do you know how to own a choo-choo train so that you can play with it whenever you want without worrying about fighting for it with other kids?"

"How?"

"Watch for the magic." BarKockalotte conjures up a piece of paper and attaches it to the caboose of the red train. "Now, Joecub owns the train exclusively. It is his private property, and he can play with it anytime he desires."

"What is the magic paper?" the little raccoon asks. "I want it too!"

"The magic paper is a deed, which is the proof of what you Have," BarKockalotte teaches with patience. "And your Love Worth has positive correlation with the deeds that you accumulate until you join the exclusive club of the Haves."

BarKockalotte attaches another deed to a green choo-choo train and allocates it to the little raccoon.

"What about me?" asks the little beaver as he approaches for another magic deed.

BarKockalotte looks around and grabs a fluffy tennis ball.

"How about a super tennis ball? It's great for playing fetch!"

"I want a tennis ball!"

"Me too!"

The two train owners try to rob the owner of his tennis ball.

"Class!" BarKockalotte barks at the unruly students. "We invented ownership so that Others respect what we Have and vice versa. Plus, if you look at your magic deeds, they all have numbers on them. The bigger, the Worthier."

The kids check one another's magic deeds.

"I don't want a tennis ball!" the three students concur based on their new knowledge learned from the canine teacher.

BarKockalotte smiles. "Smart choice," he says. "Next, let's talk about methods. How do we own things? Robbing Others is obviously not right. To Have a job, however, is the most practiced way to Have things you want. Just like education, occupation is legal, respectful, and institutionalized, so it is the least questioned way to Have."

"What is a job?" the little bear asks. "Is it a better toy than choo-choo train?"

"It is not a toy," BarKockalotte answers. "It is more of a lifestyle, if you will. It allows you to Have things."

"I want to Have a job!" the little raccoon decides.

"I want to Have things!" the little beaver adds.

"Excellent!" yelps BarKockalotte. "Where there is a will, there is a way. Next, you need to use your education to find employment. Sign a contract. They give you paychecks for toys. You give them time and Energy. Let's say I am the employer, and you are my employees. I will tell you what to do. In return, you get paid to buy the things you want."

"I do not Have a lot of time for you, but I want to Have toys."

"I do not Have Energy for you because I need to play with my toys."

"I do not like being told what to do, but I like toys."

"Aha!" BarKockalotte spots a teaching opportunity. "As long as you desire to Have, you will endure the process. You study hard in school to Have a diploma. You work hard to Have more and more things to accumulate your Love Worth. Look around my house. Are you all inspired?"

The three students shake their heads.

BarKockalotte feels deeply frustrated as an educator. He gazes with puppy eyes at the four Messengers.

"Don't look at me," Purrplexy meows. "I am a cat. I'm immune to puppy eyes."

"Don't flatter yourself," BarKockalotte woofs. "I'm seeking wisdom, not an unwitty whisker."

"I don't know," says Polisco, the newly graduated Messenger as he spelunks his right nostril. "I feel like there is a bug between what you own and what you Have. You use the two interchangeably. But ownership is an artificially invented social agreement for exclusive access to resources. In other words, ownership repels Others, thus it is Fear. If you are motivated by the desire to own, you are motivated by Fear. Am I right?"

Polisco looks at his teachers for validation.

PanRoo adds her two cents of wisdom. "I don't think there is anything wrong with Fear-motivated actions," she says. "Fear is our survival instinct. I am sure the reason that

Mr. Bar accumulates so much is to prevent unfortunate uncertainties rather than prove his Love Worth because you cannot use Fear to attract Love. Am I right?"

PanRoo also seeks validation as a fledgling Messenger.

Mr. B.V. beams like a fulfilling cultivator. He renders an elegant poem for his wisdom-thirsty students:

> the young minds want to play
> the dog works hard to Have
> all work and no play
> makes Mr. Bar a dull dog
> all play and no work
>
> ...

"I know an answer to that!" BarKockalotte howls, interrupting the beaver poet. "That is exactly why I took them to the exclusive club area. Almost all the owners here do not work. I believe it is because they have endured *all work no play* in the past to enjoy *all play no work* now. How admirable! Come on, guys. I will show you what a dream life looks like."

BarKockalotte summons the three little ones to the window to show them what a great life is like if they work hard to Have first and enjoy what they Have later. As the canine teacher and his three students stand in front of the window, they realize that the dream home has landed on a private dock of one of the luxury mansions. The Love Balloon has turned into a Fear Bubble. An army of safeguard robots point guns at them and they all shout:

"Warning! Private property, trespassing! Fire in ten seconds!"

23
Love to Have

T HE ANIMALS ARE held at gunpoint on a private dock inside the semi-transparent, membrane-like Fear Bubble. The scared children hide behind the bear couple. Purrplexy uses LeDrun as a tortoise shield while BarKockalotte barks at the weapons. Polisco and PanRoo, the two new Messengers, attempt to move the Fear Bubble away from the private property to a public park. They push, kick, and meditate with telepathic power. Nothing works. The defeated disciples turn to their mentors for help. LeDrun peels the cat off his shell and asks everyone to close their eyes. In a blink, the Fear Bubble and the animals inside disappear from the dock.

"Who farted?" asks BarKockalotte, snuffling his nose.

"Everyone," Purrplexy gags, opening her eyes. "It is a public bathroom."

"I recognize this place," says Polisco, eyeballing a crusty urinal.

"This is the sociosphere of the **D** lair," says PanRoo.

BORN RICH LEARN POOR Vol. 3

"Welcome to my big **D** lair, my friends!" LeDrun greets, levitating above the urinal.

"Really?" Mr. B.V. complains, covering his nose. "You took us from a private dock to a public bathroom?"

LeDrun winks. "I had to answer the call of Nature. It's all done now."

"What are we waiting for then?" Purrplexy urges the gang. "Let's get out of this putrid place."

PanRoo recollects something. "Wait," she says. "Didn't Mr. Bar get shot in the park last time we were here?"

BarKockalotte recollects those dark days when his eyes couldn't see well, and his goggles made him a less Worthy-looking dog. He was quite a laughingstock of the cat, who herself got burnt fur and a charred face. BarKockalotte peeks through the small, cloudy window to check the outside situation: two groups of armed animals fire at each other in the middle of the park. One group waves righteous flags to support and protect lawfully obtained Haves, while the other group flashes ethical pointers to redistributing hoarded resources from the Haves to the Have Nots. BarKockalotte feels a chill in his body and an urge to pee.

"How did this happen?" BarKockalotte barks at the window. "Where is my dream home? Where are the mansions of aspiration?"

"The Love Balloon transforms into the Fear Bubble," says LeDrun, sitting on the narrow, dusty windowsill in front of the dog, "when you switch the focus of your Energy from Having at present to maintaining the Had from the past or ensuring to Have in the future."

"I can't discern the difference," BarKockalotte whines, blowing the dust off the windowsill.

"My two cents," says Polisco, trying to craft his skills of articulating wisdom. "In the Love Balloon, your interplay with Others is Having a cocreative experience together. In the Fear Bubble, you work toward the goal to Have, like what you told the kids—study to Have a diploma, work to Have toys, that kind of shi—stuff. It's very much goal oriented. Nothing wrong with goals. But the goal is not the experience."

"With all due respect," BarKockalotte woofs with a frown, "I think there is one thing you are missing: order. In order to enjoy the Having, we need to work hard to Have first. Otherwise, how do you enjoy something that is not yours?"

"I enjoy your choo-choo train," says the little raccoon.

"Me too!" "Me too!" the other two choo-choo train fans agree.

PanRoo winks at the dog. "I also enjoy refreshing breeze, gentle sun bath, colorful foliage, and after-storm rainbows."

"Ice and snow are pretty neat, too," says the polar bear, picking his nose.

"But even squirrels save nuts for winter!" BarKockalotte feels cornered. "If we don't work hard now, how can we enjoy things later?"

"By Nature," Mr. B.V. illuminates, "the fact that squirrels save nuts is about enjoying them later. This Fear-charged action is necessary for survival. What they work hard to Have is what they will be Having. Love and Fear are in Natural harmony. On planet **F**, however, what you work hard to Have and what you will be Having are often *separated*."

"To Have and to Have more," Polisco mocks, "the **F** animals' motto."

"Then we are not as balanced as squirrels," says PanRoo. "Squirrels do not desire to Have more beyond necessity— private nuts mansions or nuts boats or nuts trust funds that last for centuries. They know that when spring comes, it is time to Love."

BarKockalotte is quiet but not convinced. He fishes around in his pocket for the strong evidence against those smart mouths.

LeDrun, from the windowsill, glances down at the dog and smiles mysteriously. He turns around and gazes through the window at the war zone outside the public bathroom. Then he chants:

> *Love is Having, Fear to Have*
> *the Virus Loves to Have*
> *Love illuminates the Essence of the Self*
> *Fear protects the Identity of the Self*
> *the Virus separates Essence from Identity*
> *Love attracts Love Energy for Love Worth*
> *Fear repels Fear Energy to prove existence*
> *the Virus replaces Love Worth with Fear proofs*
> *Love enjoys the Having at present*
> *Fear consumes Energy of the past and for the future*
> *the Virus evaluates the past and the future*
> *to judge the present*
> *Love … holy duck!*

A stray bullet hits the window and scares something out of the chanting tortoise. Startled, he jumps down from the windowsill into a urinal. Meanwhile, BarKockalotte has found his evidence—a piece of paper that says "Private Property. No Trespassing." The dog waves the warning sign and howls like a champion:

"Don't panic! This will protect us!"

The heroic dog storms out.

"I have one, too!" Joecub shouts proudly, breaking out the receipt of his choo-choo train.

"Me too!" "Me too!" The other two proud owners show off their pieces of paper.

The three young recruits follow the canine leader out.

"Wait!" PanRoo yells. "It's dangerous out there!"

"Chill," LeDrun says, crawling out of the toilet bowl. "They won't go far."

In a split second, the BarKockalotte team returns with an air of triumph.

"We are all safe now," BarKockalotte barks with conceit. "The entire park is now declared to be our private property. No one will bother u—."

Before the guard dog finishes his bark, a grenade flies in through the broken window. LeDrun jumps off the toilet and diffuses it at an uncharacteristically fast speed.

"Private my ass," Purrplexy jumps toward the door. "Get out of my way!"

BarKockalotte scuffs the frantic cat and assures: "Don't panic. I've got this."

Another hissing grenade flies in and explodes.

24
Return to Natural Experience

THE ANIMALS REGAIN their consciousness in a luxurious, palatial bathroom. While the three children explore the diamond toilets, the bear couple sits on a gold bench, reflecting the slippery slope BarKockalotte is bridging from the Nature's Sphere to his Viral Reality. LeDrun and Mr. B.V. immediately recognize this place. They camp on the ivory counter, sip the elixir from their flasks, and watch the dog. BarKockalotte, however, feels a crashing plummet of his heart, as if a powerful black bird dropped him from above the clouds to the bottom of the Racing City.

"No! This cannot be happening!" BarKockalotte barks as he storms out of the bathroom.

Everyone follows him out. They stand in the hallway and behold a modern luxury office with all red glass walls. Three golden words glitter on the office door: The Power Club. Through the glass door, the animals see an empty office and a huge desk. Looking up, they find an

AI-equipped security camera that flashes a red light as it zooms in on the dog. BarKockalotte curls up into a ball on the floor and buries his head under his tail.

"How does it smell down there?" LeDrun teases the dog. "It is not how I remember you from the last time you stood us up for your feathered lord."

Mr. B.V. recalls the incident. "That's right!" he says. "You lied about your Nature calls and informed on the Raging Rodents instead. What was your reward again?"

BarKockalotte raises his head. "I get it! I get it! It was the Virus that hijacked my Fear Energy. But I am healed now. I don't understand why we seem to lapse into the Viral Reality all over again."

"From Love to Fear," says Polisco, pressing his bear face against the glass door, "and from Fear to all Fear."

"All Fear and faux Love is the Virus," says PanRoo, holding up the dog and adjusting his face toward the camera. "Time to find out all the slippery slopes. Smile, Mr. Bar."

BarKockalotte forces a snarling smile.

The office door is open. A familiar Voice greets the dog. "Welcome to the Power Club, our model Horsezen!"

THE AMPLE OFFICE space is empty, but the glass walls are full. On the west wall are digital money figures and various currency symbols. On the east wall is a matrix of classes, ranks, rates, grades, and their corresponding Power levels. On the north wall, there are ownership deeds that reflect claims, resource allocations, and investments. And on the south wall, there are charity works and monuments. As BarKockalotte tries to discern his name on the south wall, the Voice says to him:

"Mr. Bar, welcome to the Club! I knew you would be back. Take the Power Seat, please. You have earned the privilege."

The empty chair behind the office desk swivels to beckon its new commander.

"I'll take it!" Joecub is intrigued by the swiveling chair and volunteers to take the Power Seat.

"What a promising young man!" the Voice praises. "In the Power Seat, you are privileged to Have anything you want."

"I want to Have all the toys in the world!" Joecub commands.

"You Have them now," the Voice says.

Joecub looks around the empty office. "Where are they?"

"It is impossible to accommodate all the toys in the world in one room," the Voice laughs, "but you own all the toy stocks. Here is your portfolio."

A folder appears on the desk of the confused all-toy-owner.

"I want all toys!" "I want all the toys!" the two other young toy lovers rush to the toy king and try to overthrow him from the throne.

"Mr. Bar!" the Voice shouts at the dog. "Enforce law and order!"

"Guys," BarKockalotte woofs. "Rules are rules. Joecub claimed all the toy resources first. Respect that."

"However," says the Voice, raising itself, "you two can

work for him. Use your time and Energy in exchange for toys."

"I'll give you ten toys a week for your time and Energy," says Joecub to the little raccoon. "And one toy a week for yours," he says, turning to the little beaver.

"Why? That's unfair!" the little beaver protests.

"Because she is my new sister," Joecub shrugs, leaning back in the Seat. "And I own all the toys. You don't have to work for me. Thousands of other kids would be glad to."

"Haha!" the Voice laughs with satisfaction. "That is right. With all the toys in the world, you can attract endless friends. THAT is your Love Worth."

The little beaver weeps.

BarKockalotte kneels to comfort the low-paid kid: "Hey, don't cry. Look up and aspire to the sky! You could get promoted to two toys weekly, then three, four, and all the way to ten, given proper training, credentials, hard work, and networking. Your little raccoon friend can be your aspiration to reach that destination. Step by step, your life is full of hope!"

The little beaver somehow feels hopelessly motivated.

PanRoo gazes at her conceited son and feels remotely proud. She asks LeDrun and Mr. B.V., who are camping on the desk and drinking: "I would like to take on a challenge. I know that is BarKockalotte's Virus, but I want to try the Seat."

Polisco stops his audacious bear partner. "I don't think it's a good idea," he says. "You just became a Messenger. How do you know Bark-A-Lot's Virus won't reinfect you? Stay clear, my dear."

"You are enlightened," says LeDrun, stowing his purple

crystal flask in his shell, "when you see your own Virus inside and cultivate the true Self out of the Viral Reality. You are a Messenger when you illuminate and help cultivate Others. So go ahead, Messenger PanRoo."

With Polisco and Barkockalotte's forceful assistance, Joecub steps down with a pouty face and swears to return.

"Ms. PanRoo," the Voice greets the new commander in the Seat of Power, "you can Have anything you want, just like men."

"If women are like men, are men like women?" PanRoo asks the Virus. "If I can Have anything I want, what do I give for what I Have?"

"You don't need to give anything, Ms. PanRoo."

"Then I will not Have anything because that is a lie," says PanRoo. "You distract by dangling the goal in front of us while stealing our Energy from our present life experience, which is the true Value of the Self and the Legacy with Others."

"Master Pan," BarKockalotte whimpers helpfully, "all the things you Have will turn into your Love Worth that attracts Others to Love you!"

"It is the same light that shines and reflects between the Self and Others," says PanRoo in the Chair. "The way you evaluate your Self Worth is the way you evaluate Others. I Love you not because of what you Have. It is what we Have together. You share new lights, new air, new possibilities, and new experiences with me that enrich my life. You are Worthy as much my Love Energy as you radiate it out, Mr. Bar."

BarKockalotte is quiet with watery eyes.

"Power, Power," Mr. B.V. says, petting the dog

affectionately. "To craft a slippery slope from Nature's Sphere into the Viral Reality, the Social Virus always invites Power to the show."

"And *separation* is always the first slippery slope," Polisco adds while keeping order of the three youngsters.

"Yes," LeDrun says, levitating in midair. "The first slippery slope to the Viral Reality is always *separation* so that the Virus can build its Power Center in the gap. In BarKockalotte's case, it is the separation of *experience* from *goal*, thus Truth from Reality, Self from Others. In Nature's Sphere, the experience and the goal are one. Experience is Natural as your Energy interacts with other Energy and causes wave patterns inside you. A goal results from innate desires or social needs to measure, control, bring about, or curtail certain outcomes. However, intelligent animals on planet **F** invented ownership that is used by many as their goal to accumulate the proof of Have—calculable, comparable, and legally protected, but devoid of experience."

"So, Having is like experience whereas to Have is like a goal," says Polisco in contemplation. "When separated, the achievement of the goal must feel empty."

LeDrun continues the enlightenment. "Second, *replacement*," he intones. "Taking advantage of the separation, the Social Virus inculcates more artificial social inventions to replace Natural experience—ownership, credential, award, income, class, privilege, entitlement, exclusive access, profit, stock, etc. Take the **F** animals' life path prescription as an example. Educational backgrounds have replaced wisdom and knowledge; occupations and income replaced social Value and Self Worth; awards replaced qualities; levels replaced capabilities; ranks replaced influences; and so forth. It is an artificial construct where life is a buildable project with goals and achievements. Once separated and replaced, the Virus successfully settles in the victim's mind for further indoctrination and exploitation."

"Third, *Power*," LeDrun continues. "The Virus then invites Power to accelerate the path down the slippery slope into the Viral Reality. Power is the judgment of achievement—success or failure, big or small, high or low, great or lesser, Worthy or Worthless, significant or trifling, distinguishable or negligible and so on. The primary role of Viral Power is to reorient its subjects by telling them where they should concentrate their Energy—Fear Energy, of course because Love neither sets goals nor judges the achievements. Love bonds and enjoys the experience. At this point, the Social Virus has finished building its Power Center to lord its victims."

"As you all know," Mr. B.V. adds, "the monster's ultimate trick is to disguise Fear as Love so that it can motivate the victim with Fear and artificial lure that appears like Love."

"Last, *pursuit of Power*," says LeDrun. "In Nature's Sphere, Love and Fear flow in harmony. *Love gives way to Fear when in danger; Fear gives way to Love when safe.* In Viral Reality, the Social Virus conditions its victims to expend constant Fear Energy to accumulate their **F** Worth. It is Fear because **F** Worth is not about experiential cocreation. It is all about calculatable accumulation. *Rich is a Natural growth experience; Poor is a Virus conditioned mindset.*"

"BORN RICH LEARN POOR," says Mr. B.V., smiling at BarKockalotte. "You were born with tremendous Love Worth. The more you own, the less you are Worthy."

The two new Messengers enlighten the dog: "*Unlearn* to save the children."

BarKockalotte walks to the Power Seat. He picks up the swivel chair and smashes it through the wall of the red glass office.

BARKOCKALOTTE WAVES THE long-handled wood splitter with the determination to break apart the toy box. Joecub, in anticipation of playing with his choo-choo train, cheers on the dog. The rest of the animals stay away from the snarling dog. With a big crackling sound, the toy box collapses into a toy pile.

"My choo-choo train!" Joecub sits atop the pile, holding the train tightly to his chest.

"What makes it yours?" BarKockalotte asks the bear cub. "Did you invent it? Did you design it? Did you produce it? Did you distribute it? Do you understand how it runs? Can you fix it when it breaks? Can you see the Self in all the Others I mentioned?"

Joecub frowns, examining the empty train. "It is a small train for so many things."

"Then how do you connect the Self with Others through the train?" BarKockalotte asks the disheartened child encouragingly.

Joecub's eyes sparkle. "I can be a choo-choo train cab driver!"

The little raccoon waves her paw. "I could use a cab."

"Where to, Madam?" Joecub asks his first passenger.

"The Sanctuary."

25

The Company Jingle

I T IS A chilly Saturday morning. The bear couple sits by the pool in the backyard to watch their two children rehearsing for the company jingle audition. Polisco leisurely rolls a booger ball with his stubby fingers while complaining about the drying air in fall that hardens and bloodies his nose elixir. PanRoo stows the tablet in her pouch and takes off her headset.

"I have deep concerns about Jo," says PanRoo. "His infection seems to get worse. The nightmares of the mind monster visit him more and more frequently. Yesterday, he told me that the monster asked him to eat his sister's brain and then Em's, his best friend from school. We joined this Messenger cultivation program to be Rich, and more important, to save our child. Why do I feel that we are doing him a disservice?"

"The slippery slopes are tricky," says Polisco, rolling the booger ball meditatively. "Even though our intent is Love, if we do not stay truthful to the Self and mindful of Others, then at some point, we may still fall for the mind trick that the Virus plays. How do you think our cub got acquainted with the mind monster?"

"Essential Legacy versus Viral Legend," says PanRoo in contemplation. "I hope Jo flourishes in our Love, not be haunted by our Virus. Maybe that is the real reason LeDrun and Mr. B.V. cultivate us. I am not an evader, but I don't think we are the only animals who have introduced him to the mind monster. Purrplexy is obsessed with the company jingle and the rendition of it by kids. I can hear the Voice in the jingle."

"Purrplexy has her own cultivation journey," says Polisco, throwing the booger ball into PanRoo's pouch. "Messengers may illuminate, but the enlightenment comes from inside. Plus, I am quite entertained by the two singing talents. Joecub grunts like a pooping bugle call. I think I need to take a dump."

"My enlightened Messenger," PanRoo teases Polisco, "I wonder when you will host the farewell party to your childish booger bombs, potty jokes, and farty pranks. I am more than happy to throw the party for you. It will be called 'Bon Voyage, Discharges!'"

"But they are the best part," Polisco argues. "The Rich are childish. The wise are unlearned. The discharges are Natural. The polar bear needs to answer to the bugle call."

Purrplexy uncharacteristically gets up early for the audition. She straightens her fur, wears light makeup, puts on a professional suit dress, and drags the sleepy dog off the bed to assist her grandiose marketing project—auditioning young talents for the brand-new company ad jingle. Purrplexy, the marketing director, asks her canine assistant to set up the stage, the cameras, microphones, and lighting while enjoying her first cup of catnip coffee.

"How many candidates do we have?" BarKockalotte woofs, adjusting the tripod.

"Three," Purrplexy meows, checking the script of the jingle.

"I think I can name them all: a little bear, a little raccoon, and a little beaver. You're the cheapest cat I've ever known."

Purrplexy is embarrassed. "You don't think I want to run a worldwide promotion?" she says. "We're a small startup, and the stupid new ownership cut our budget due to the three-year-old hippo's traumatic experience with robots. I had to use free AI to compose our jingle and then use social media to promote it. I am the most pathetic marketing director in the world."

BarKockalotte tilts his dog head. "AI jingle?" he asks. "Is it original? Who's the artist?"

"I am," says Purrplexy, licking her paw. "I put in some keywords and desired emotional reactions. Voila! Dozens of ad jingles were generated. Easy pawsy."

"I see," BarKockalotte snarls. "A cheap marketer *and* a creative cheat."

"Whatever," says Purrplexy, dismissing the dog's deriding remarks. "I think the jingle will be a hit. It goes like this: The Cheerleader Robots Will Never Let You Down! Do you get it? The robots cheer you up, so they never let you down. Clever, isn't it?"

"It doesn't sound too shabby," BarKockalotte nods. "But I don't see the necessity of running a promotion. It is too early. Our product is not yet off the ground. What are you trying to sell? A promise?"

"A Legend." Purrplexy gives the marketing fool a side-eye. "I am building the Legend of our company. You don't wait for the product. You want to start telling the story now. A good story is everything. It decides the popularity of our product, the Value of our brand, and the Legend of our company."

"Nonsense," BarKockalotte woofs. "No matter how good a story is, no product, no Value. No Legacy, no Legend."

"Listen up," says Purrplexy, raising her voice, "I don't give a rat's ass about your dorky dog world, but in our majestic feline kingdom, we have something called *purrsona*. It is like the Legend of a cat. Every cat has a story. And cats with the most popular stories are honored with paw prints with their names embedded in the glorious Avenue of Catwalk of Fame. It is every cat's dream. However, to be super popular, you must tell a killer story about your Self. Similarly, if you want to have a popular product, you need to tell a killer story about your company."

BarKockalotte raises his eyebrow. "Why would I want to be popular?"

"Who doesn't?" Purrplexy laughs in contempt. "To feel Loved and Valued by many? Not to feel lonely or left out? To be a star and make a ton?"

"So, popularity is the soil for profitability," BarKockalotte mocks.

"The key to success, fame, and Legend," Purrplexy

corrects the argumentative dog. "And marketing is the art of telling that killer story."

"In that case, marketing genius," BarKockalotte teases the feline marketing director, "good luck with your candidates today. We all know how talented they are. The cub grunts like a bear with constipation. The little raccoon screams like an off-tune siren. And the little beaver whistles like a broken chainsaw."

"Which century are you from?" asks Purrplexy, laughing at the outdated dog. "We can always post-produce the audio to make it sound perfect. What we need are the children's cheerful faces and innocent smiles. Let the expert take care of rest."

"Knock! Knock!" Someone is at the front door.

"Get the door," says BarKockalotte. "Your little broken chainsaw and his grandpa are here."

Mr. B.V. takes his grandkit to the conference room for the audition. Joecub and his foster sister grunt and scream in the backyard, warming up vocally for the upcoming audition. Purrplexy makes the candidate watch the jingle demo for the final preparation. The little beaver practices for a while and then approaches the feline marketing director with a question.

"What do these words mean?" the little beaver asks.

"They mean good things, Sweetie," Purrplexy smiles. "All you need to do is smile wide and sing those words in front of the camera. You will have a chance to become our company's youngest brand ambassador."

The little beaver is more perplexed. "What is brand amb—ass—a, what is brand?"

"Brand is …" Purrplexy tries to cultivate the young mind. "Are you a cool kid in school?"

"I don't know," the little beaver says with a frown. "I need to ask my classmates."

"How your classmates feel about you," Purrplexy nurtures, "is how buyers perceive a brand. Marketing helps a brand look cool by telling stories."

"Why?" The beaver does not follow.

"Because cool kids are popular kids," Purrplexy smiles. "And cool brands are popular brands. In fact, some brands are so popular on planet F that they dominate our lives. How powerful!"

BarKockalotte has millions of counterarguments against the cat. Before he can organize his thoughts and words, the two young siblings in the backyard get into another fight. The little bear roars, pushing the little raccoon into the swimming pool. The canine babysitter rushes out of the conference room and drags the soaked raccoon out of the water. As they shake off and return, the parents bearhandle the culprit cub in the conference room for an interrogation.

"Joecub!" Polisco calls his son's full name. "Why did you push your sister into the pool?"

"She won't shut up!" says Joecub. "She keeps asking me 'How do we know? How do we know for sure?' I do not care! I just want to be on TV!"

"How do we know what, Honeycoon?" PanRoo asks the little raccoon.

"The jingle," says the little raccoon. "We are supposed to sing 'The Cheerleader Robots Will Never Let You Down.'

But how do we know? I've never met a cheerleader robot. What if it does let you down sometimes? Does it mean that we are lying? I do not want to say things that I don't understand anymore. My mom used to make me say all kinds of things in front of the camera that I didn't understand. It made me sick. I blacked out a lot. The doctor said I had Star Syndrome."

"Who cares?" Jo yells at his doubtful sister. "We will be on TV!"

"I want to be on TV!" the little beaver cheers.

Purrplexy corrects the children's expectations. "It's online," she says. "But the virtual space is even better for telling stories. And your kids are the best story tellers! Who doesn't trust your innocent eyes and sincere smiles? I do! Are you ready to be stars? Let's line up and jingle!"

Motivated by the seasoned marketing director, the little raccoon joins the promotion. Purrplexy turns on the camera, adjusts the lighting, arranges the candidates on the stage, and begins the audition. The entire Star Valley hears a grunting bear cub, a screaming raccoon kitten, and a vrooming beaver chainsaw when the music comes on. The proud parents put on headsets and discreetly switch the mode to noise canceling. The loving beaver grandpa goes to the bathroom and does not come out. Even the supportive dog sits by the swimming pool in the backyard for a water break. Among the raging animal parade, LeDrun meditates on the coffee table in the living room and chants:

Love attracts via Essential originality
Fear repels through mass-produced popularity
Love illuminates individual novelty
Fear issues standards for the vast majority

Love inspires artistic creation
Fear maintains necessities through mass production
Love sheds light on the Essence of the Self
through the reflection of Others
Fear conceals the Essence
with a veneer of stories of the Self
for popular attention
Love transforms your Essence into a Legacy
that lives on in Others after you return to the Origin
Fear manufactures a fiction called the Self
to deceive Others for Essence preservation

Bang! Bang! Bang! Suddenly, someone kicks the front door. The professional animals, however, are so busy singing or taking refuge from the company jingle that nobody senses the approaching danger.

With a metal-against-metal sound clash, the front door is kicked open. The porcupine neighbor across the street stands tall at the door. He puts his gun back into his holster and shouts at the shocked animals:

"What's going on here? Are you slaughtering animals? Keep it down!"

Purrplexy crosses her arms. "We are auditioning young talents for our company jingle," she announces proudly.

"For real? I'll fetch my little brother right now. By the way, you need a new lock for the front door."

26
Promised Land

THE BIG OVER-ARMED porcupine escorts his little brother to the company jingle audition in the conference room. The little porcupine sings better than a world-famous nightingale pop star and dances more impressively than a blue-footed booby. The other three little candidates are initially in awe and then begin feeling insecure. Purrplexy, the marketing director, gazes into the little porcupine's eyes and signals him to stop.

"Thanks for coming," Purrplexy says, turning off the camera.

"He is the winner, isn't he?" the big porcupine asks confidently.

"Due to the large quantity of applications," the cat director answers professionally, "we can only inform the winner. We will contact you if the applicant is chosen."

"Bullshit!" the big porcupine yells at the cat. "My little brother is the most talented porcupine I have ever known!

Make the three imbeciles perform again. I'll judge them myself!"

"Sir," BarKockalotte, the company security officer barks at the self-invited porcupines. "We must ask you two to leave."

"Make them sing again, right now!" the big porcupine says, taking out his gun and holding it to Purrplexy's head.

BarKockalotte backs off, subconsciously touching a scar on his forehead, thanks to this porcupine who hit him with a barbed quill drumstick not long ago.

"Okay! Okay!" Purrplexy raises her front paws. "Your little brother won! Congratulations!"

"Brother, please!" the little porcupine begs. "They took care of me when our late big brother accidentally shot our late father."

"You shut your mouth!" the big porcupine hisses, retracting the weapon. "Now, since my little brother is the jingle winner, let's talk about compensation. I am his agent."

"Well," Purrplexy stutters with flattened ears. "Our company is more of uh … p—platform for the young talents. Once the jingle is released, your little brother will become a huge star. The money will flood in, I promise."

"Promise is my favorite thorn," says the big porcupine, spinning his gun on his index finger. "You know what a promise is? It is a *debt* to collect. Guess what I do for a living? I'm a professional debt collector, and I never fail because I either take your money or take your life. I'll leave my little brother here for now. Remember, I will come back to collect on that debt. If you don't keep your promise, you won't get to keep your life."

The thorny debt collector waves his gun at all the animals and then struts out.

The moment the big porcupine disappears, Joecub screams at the little porcupine: "Follow your big brother and get out of my house! It is *my* jingle for *my* company! I do not want to hear you singing or see you dancing because I am the best, better than the rest!"

"But he wants me to stay," the little porcupine says through his tears. "He will kill me if I don't listen to him!"

"I don't care! Get out of my house!"

The bear cub throws another world-class temper tantrum on the floor.

Purrplexy, the initiator of the whole thing, sits in the director's chair, motionless, petrified. She does not hear Joecub's ear-piercing scream. She does not respond to BarKockalotte's barks about how violent and dangerous that big porcupine is. She cannot answer the bear couple's question on how she will keep her promise. She will not react to the other two non-chosen young animals' plead to sing the jingle anyway. All she can think of is how to keep her life. She wishes she could go back to the past and shut her big cat mouth. She wishes she had never promised anything to a dangerous debt collector or to anybody in general because she has no clue how to keep a promise. All she wants now is a box to hide in. Oh box! Sparks light up her sinking heart in the dark. Purrplexy meows at the magic tortoise for help.

THE I RESORT in Purrplexy's mind is a promised land full
of fairy tales. In the hallway of the luxury resort, a big
screen welcomes the distinguished guests and promises
them a luxurious, relaxing, and happy experience. Endless
commercials follow digital greetings—food commercials
promise you a satisfying experience with quick meals of
great deals; automobile commercials promise you a fast
experience that defies other drivers and traffic laws; entertainment commercials promise you a dramatic experience
that involves laughter and tears, romance and violence;
insurance commercials promise you a safe and secure
experience in unlikely life scenarios endorsed by likely or
not so much celebrities; medicine commercials promise
you a healthy life experience with aspiring lifestyle slide-
shows and glossed over lethal side effects. It is a fairyland
that promises its believers a perfectly prefabricated real-life
experience.

Purrplexy proudly leads the animals into an aroma-in-
fused elevator with well-dressed mouse operators. The
elevator takes the dazzled animals, especially the young
ones, to the fan-shaped Love Terrace. Unlike the consum-
eristic lobby, the Terrace is packed with animals talking,
singing, and pantomiming to their phones. The whole
place is as loud and bubbly as a pot of boiling water, but no
single drop directly interacts with others nearby. Purrplexy
sits on the marble floor, sweeping her tail and purring.

"I know what you all are thinking," says the cat. "My
Love Balloon will *not* kick me out this time."

"Enlighten me," BarKockalotte woofs. "Why did you
get ejected last time? And how is this time different?"

"I've learned my lesson," says Purrplexy, cleaning her

face. "You cannot keep Having without Giving. Last time, I wanted to Have all the catnip in the world, which was unrealistic and unsustainable. After contemplating on it, I have become enlightened about how Love is about Giving. Look around this place. Everybody is busy Giving. Rich is not about accumulating what you Have but about what you Give. What you Give decides your Love Value and builds your Legend."

"I don't know," says PanRoo. "Love as the Essential Force of Attraction happens between two parties and enriches both. Does what you Give carry your Essence? And when you Give, who is on the other end to Receive? If it does not resonate with the Receiver, how do you know what you Give holds Value?"

"If I were the Love Balloon," BarKockalotte woofs, "with your tarnished record, I wouldn't take you on another trip."

"Well, I believe in second chances!" Purrplexy hisses. "If you all keep quiet and do not distract me, I will show you how forgiving my Love Balloon is."

All the wise mouths are shut. Purrplexy closes her eyes and purrs out her Love Message. A Love Balloon with a box gondola hanging below slowly and hesitantly lands on the Terrace.

PURRPLEXY'S LOVE BALLOON is full of recording equipment, post-production studios, and media platforms. The young talents immediately turn it into their playground. The little porcupine twirls around the microphone stand and sings like a pop star; the little bear cub moves his hips and pouts his lips in front of the camera like a cyber star; the little beaver whittles a wood block into a trophy like an arts and crafts star; and the little raccoon tags different platforms as "recyclables" and "pure trash" like a social movement star. Purrplexy, the director, gathers the little galvanized animals and the forbearing adults for a meeting.

"Guys," says Purrplexy, "let's make a new jingle for the company. Fruck AI! Pardon my Felinench. Both intelligence and creativity originate from our Essence, not Artificiality."

Mr. B.V. winks at the cat. "That sounds illuminating," he says. "Isn't your robot product AI-powered?"

"I don't care!" Purrplexy yowls at the beaver. "This is my Love Balloon, so I am the leader. The new jingle should tell the Essential story of our company. And our company is comprised of the bonded Love Balloons of all of us. Who wants to cocreate the company jingle with me?"

"Count me in!" Polisco raises his paw. "I have held onto my longtime passion for entrepreneurship. I can turn it into a melody. I was the keyboard player for my band in high school."

"I am crafty with words," says PanRoo, joining the mission. "I'll weave the most eloquent and genuine lyrics into your melody."

"I'll take care of the scripts for the jingle video!" BarKockalotte howls skywards. "I have always dreamed of being a creative writer!"

"Excellent! I will direct," Purrplexy acclaims. Turning to the young talents, she adds, "There will be no auditions nor promises for anything. But if you hear the new jingle and Love it, please join us. Remember, *everybody is an artist when in Love.*"

The four young minds do not quite understand the words, but they can feel the cocreative Energy.

Then the cocreation begins. The bonded animals have access to each other's Essence and Energy. They share, listen, understand, debate, align, integrate, craft, finesse, and generate. Through Love, the Essential Force of Attraction, they see one another's Essence as complementary talents contributing to cocreation. Through bonding, they share each other's Energy that flows in as inspiration, motivation, aspiration, and strength. The new jingle embodies everyone's Essence and carries their Legacy. Upon release, all the young talents Love it and resonate with it. They sing, dance, and laugh together in the jingle video. Their sheer joy is so captivating that the adult creators join them. As they enjoy the sweet fruit of their cocreation effort, a purple thought creeps into the feline marketing director's mind.

27
The Cat's Love Value

URRPLEXY WATCHES THE joyous, creative animals singing, dancing, laughing, and goofing off in her Love Balloon. A thought appears in her mind like a purple lightning bolt in the dark sky. She turns off all the equipment and stands before the audience like a motivational speaker with a question mark tail.

"Teammates!" Purrplexy meows passionately. "Now that our company story is released on all platforms, are you all anxious to see the stats?"

"I want to see the stars!" the youngsters chorus like four enthusiastic fans.

BarKockalotte pops the bubble. "She meant statistics," he barks. "Numbers, rates, ranks, percentages, you know, the math stuff you study in school."

"Eww," the schoolers have a sudden loss of appetite.

"No, no," Purrplexy meows, leering at the dog. "Math is boring, but stats are fascinating because they tell you how well you have told your story—how many animals like it, discuss it, debate it, share it, promote it. They are indicators of the Love Value of our company."

"Love what?" "What Value?" the bear couple asks.

"Love Value," Purrplexy answers, gazing into the sky, "is the influence of what we Give in other animals' lives. It is our Legend."

"Hold on a second," PanRoo stops the cat, "I thought we were all aware of the end of Love. It is when calculation, evaluation, comparison, competition, classification, and categorization overtake passion, inspiration, connection, compassion, interdependence, and cocreation. The stats are the loud and clear signals of knowing, not experiencing; of evaluating, not creating. Thus, Love does not live in stats. As for Value, it is a little presumptuous to decide the Value of what you Give unilaterally, don't you think?"

"Not at all," Purrplexy shrugs. "Stats are the most efficient way to know the Love Value you Give and Receive. For instance, students know the Love Value of the education they Receive through the rankings of the schools. In the same fashion, graduates know the Love Value they Give to society with the education they Receive from such schools. Employees know the Love Value of what they Give at work based on the compensation they Receive. Business owners know the Love Value of their products or services through the sales they achieve and the profits they reap. Consumers know the Love Value of their purchase based on how much they spend. Stars know the Love Value of their personal brands based on the numbers of their fans and the fees for their time. Love Value relies on telling a great story to attract as many as possible. In other words, popularity is the key to building our Legend."

"What if," BarKockalotte woofs with a frown, "the story does not gain popularity? What if only a few like our company jingle?"

"Great question!" Purrplexy meows with excitement. "You're not too dumb a dog after all. If the story does not attract the desired outcome, you change it. That is the magic of storytelling. Although this is my first time being a marketing director, I assure you that telling a popular story of a company is not that different from telling a story of your Self. I rule this domain. For instance, the initial story of my purrsona was a cat yoga guru from a remote, exotic place. I even did the accent. But it did not cause a ripple in the virtual vast ocean online. So, I changed my story to a thought leader of kindness and compassion who had survived paper bag traumas and spray bottle abuse. That was a good strategy because female thought leaders are rising in feline communities. My new purrsona gained popularity quickly. I have published three books, own a website with many blogs, online courses, training programs, and all the social media posts to share everything. I am now a real Legend!"

"Kindness and compassion?" BarKockalotte laughs. "You're the most unkind, insensitive cat I have ever known."

"It is about what I Give, not who I am!" Purrplexy hisses at the laughing dog.

"How do you find time to create all the content?" aks PanRoo, wide eyed.

"Easy," Purrplexy winks. "You know me. I've always hated reading and writing. It's fatally boring. So, I hire animals—ghostwriters, content creators, copywriters, and so forth. Oh, and my new favorite is AI."

"So, you are a feline fraud," says Polisco, sniffing his freshly-scented fingers.

Purrplexy rolls her eyes. "I am a successful storyteller! Even the President has his speeches written! Give me a break."

"Easy, tiger," PanRoo says, stopping the cat's zoomies. "Just one quick question—do your purrsonas tell true stories of who you are? Are they real?"

"Well," says Purrplexy with a shrug, "define *true* and define *real*. If nobody Loves you and Values you when you tell the truth, I say don't bother because it is meaningless. On the contrary, even if your stories are not quite true, but everybody Loves them and Values you for them, I say it is as real as it gets. Stars do not tell true stories of themselves in movies and TV shows. But can you deny the reality of their fame and fortune due to those stories? They are all Legends that go down in history. The examples might be extreme, but we all do it to some extent."

"Speak for yourself," says PanRoo in contemplation. "I think Truth has something to do with our Essence and Reality aligning with our Identity. But if we don't tell a True story of the Self, we risk separating our Essence from our Identity, which is the very first slippery slope toward Viral Reality."

"Suit yourself," Purrplexy dismisses. "I choose to build my Legend. On the journey, stats are my flashlight, popularity is the key." She turns to the four young minds for followship.

"Who wants to be popular?" Purrplexy asks the young-sters just like a thought leader.

"Me!Me!Me!Me!" the four future leaders shout and jump.

"I want to be popular!" says the little bear cub. "When you are popular at school, nobody will call you names like Panda Ears."

"I want to be popular!" says the little raccoon. "When you are popular at school, nobody thinks you are a weirdo because you have blackouts."

"I want to be popular!" says the little porcupine. "When you are popular at school, nobody will avoid you because your brothers are ex-cons."

"I want to be popular!" says the little beaver. "When you are popular at school, nobody will bully you and call you a nerd."

"Exactly!" Purrplexy exclaims. "We all want to be popular for our own reasons. You are young and promising. There are plenty of life decisions waiting ahead of you. Do you want to know the secret to having a bright future? It is what I call *popularity attracts popularity*—choose a hot major in college, find a sought-after career, wear fashionable brands, and listen to popular music. Popular animals? Befriend them. Popular shows? Watch them. Popular events? Attend them. Popular groups? Support them. Popular sites? Visit them. Viral videos? Watch them. Trending topics? Check them. Popular purrsonas? Become them. The list is long. But the golden nugget is that popularity attracts popularity."

The four young minds absorb the cat teacher's words like a sponge soaking up water.

"I have some golden nuggets for ya," Polisco smirks at the cat, wrinkling up his nose as if he smelled something poopish. "Sameness does not attract like a magnet. It amasses like a black hole. When we are Loved, we are Loved for our unique Essence from inside. Popularity, however, is a collective phenomenon from outside. In other words, popularity could be Real but not True because Truth is outbound from the intrinsic Essence whereas Reality is inbound from extrinsic contexts. When what you Give does not generate from your Essence or resonate with Others, there is no Love Value. Your popularity-oriented life decisions will consume your Energy but will not build your Legacy. When the Death Messenger returns your Essence to the Origin after you die, at best, you will leave nothing that is uniquely you to the world, and at worst, you'll infect those who trust you unconditionally. Right? Bulbous Head? Orange Teeth?"

With no intention of joining the debate, the two Messengers laugh while playing a drinking game in one of the production studios.

"I agree with Pol," says PanRoo with a frown. "Love is the Essential Force of Attraction between two bonded parties, which means Love happens simultaneously between Give and Receive, source and sink, positive and negative. Popularity does not attract popularity. It results in atrophy. Just look at the **F** society."

"What's atrophy?" Purrplexy meows. "Sorry, you lost me at source and sink. Is it a sexual innuendo? Because sink could be, you know." The cat makes a loose fist. "And the source could be, you know." She gives the middle claw.

"I agree with master Pan," the dog howls skyward, shutting up the cat. "Worth and Value are one, like breathing in and out. Ownership has nothing to do with Love Worth because Love Worth is Having a shared experience that enriches both at present, whereas ownership seals a past transaction and ensures future access. Similarly, storytelling has nothing to do with Love Value because Love Value is cocreated between the Giver and Receiver at present, whereas storytelling narrates past events or future fictions, my dear friend."

"Don't you ever dear friend me, you flunky dog!" Purrplexy puffs up, feeling cornered. "Who doesn't want the kids to be popular at school? Just look at these beautiful children! They are the future of our planet!"

The bear couple hears some reasonable things about what the cat has to say but they are unsure, so they turn to their mentors for advice. However, the magic tortoise and the beaver bend their legs and hold their heads with their eyes closed.

"Brace yourself. We will be ejected into the high sky again," the two wise animals warn.

28
Past, Stories, Future

URRPLEXY'S BOX-SHAPED GONDOLA plummets from the high sky like a tumbling reentry capsule from outer space. Maybe because the animals' desperate screams scare the box, perhaps because it is designed to transform when in danger, as it approaches the surface of the crater lake, it turns into a semi-transparent, membrane-like Fear Bubble. Large screens have replaced the recording equipment and postproduction studios inside the original Love Balloon. The Fear Bubble floats down like a parachute and lands safely on water. The rest of the animals celebrate the feat of a water landing. Purrplexy, however, stares at a screen, oblivious to the change.

"Wow, that was close!" BarKockalotte barks his heart out, tail between his legs. "I blacked out in the sky, thanks to my acrophobia. Wait, this place looks bizarrely familiar!"

"Because this is where your doghouse is," Polisco grins, pointing to a bone-shaped doghouse attached to an orange bouncing balloon.

BarKockalotte inhales deeply with shocked eyes "No way!" he howls. "Have we time-traveled into the past? But I don't accumulate Love Worth anymore. I am an enlightened dog!"

"Or the future," PanRoo points out. "Ask the cat culprit. It was her Love Balloon that kicked us all the way here right after she boasted about the children and the future."

Purrplexy looks around. "What are you talking about? I don't see any difference around here. What doghouse? Not that I want to see it."

"They are right there!" The four young animals push the cat closer to the semi-transparent Fear Bubble wall and guide her glance toward the doghouse.

Now the dog diagnoses the cat. "Maybe she had a concussion," he reasons. "And you know, a concussion could cause vision problems."

"I did not have a concussion!" Purrplexy yowls. "I simply don't care what's going on out there. Too many senseless animals make too much noise in the world."

"How do you know what to Give if you don't care?" asks BarKockalotte. "More important to you, how do you know if your story gains popularity?"

"Again, stats, stats, stats," says Purrplexy, pointing to the screens on the wall. "I have all the information I need right in front of me—vivid, accurate, substantial, and updated."

"I see," Polisco says. "You live in the past. You rely on past data, past events, past knowledge, past experiences, past reports, and past records to tell a past story of who you are and what you Give to the world. There is nothing wrong with relying on the past because the past can protect us. It is what Fear uses to take safety precautions. However, it is not where Love lives to attract, bond, cocreate, and mutually enrich. A past story does not Give Love Value of the present."

"On the contrary," Purrplexy meows, "I live in the future, not the past. I only look forward, never look back. I draw vision boards. I dream high. I aspire to the mountains and oceans. I aim for the stars and paint rainbow roads to the promised land in the sky."

"I see," PanRoo says with a smile. "But living in the future entails living in the past at the moment you linearize the two polarities from the spherical presence called *now*. A well-rounded life experience is stretched into a life story with a timeline. There is nothing wrong with living in the future, but the future is not where Love lives to illuminate your Essence and share your Legacy. It is what Fear uses to escape the present."

"Did you hear that?" BarKockalotte howls with excitement. "Neither the past nor the future is about Love. The past is recorded, whereas the future is projected. They both happen in our minds, where time tricks us. Records are modifiable. Projections are manipulatable. If we are unaware of this trick, we are easily fooled by our mind."

Purrplexy frowns. "I'm no fool," she says. "Stories are meant to attract attention, not report the facts. The F animals are obsessed with stories because we live in a future-oriented culture—we project our lives based on life expectancies. We borrow from the future with credit cards, mortgages, and loans. We set goals to achieve in the near and far future. We work hard toward a great future. We raise kids to give them a bright future. We invest for a profitable future. Our stock market reacts to the future. We design the future. We plan the future. We control the future. We ruin the present in the name of a better future. Had it not been for the future fever, we would not have had our startup funded in the first place. Analyze that, entrepreneurs."

All the adult animals are silent. BarKockalotte whines several times to fill the awkward silence but shuts his mouth when he sees the masters' solemn faces. The four clueless children imprint their faces on the membrane-like wall of the Fear Bubble, fascinated by the vast crater lake and the surrounding mountains. Beneath their feet, however, the Bubble cracks, and a red monster swooshes in like lightning, lighting up the Bubble with a Viral red glow. The crack enlarges. The breathable Fear Bubble boundary hardens.

BarKockalotte finally organizes his thoughts for a counterargument. "I beg to differ," he woofs. "I think the F animals enjoy stories because we live in a past-oriented culture. We rely on past data, experiences, information, and technologies to know most things, do most things, and make the most decisions. We teach our children past knowledge in schools. We use our past education and past work experience to find jobs. We report past events and share past images on media. We consume what has already been made and follow what we have already established. We identify ourselves with names from the past. We see other animals in the light of the past. We know the world through past stats and stories. We believe in the past. We hold on to the past. We package the present into the box of the past and label it *for sale*."

"Future culture!" "Past culture!" "You stink!" "You suck!" The dog and the cat engage in another civil debate.

"Quiet!" PanRoo separates the two brawling animals. "What are you arguing about? You are talking about the same thing. The past and future are both Fear-charged linear thought spaces, designed by Nature to protect our Love-charged spherical being. I would say that our **F** culture is both a future-oriented culture and a past-oriented culture because it is a Fear culture. We use the ladder of the past to grasp the light of the future at the expense of the present. We trust data but discredit intuitions. We study knowledge but are ignorant of our emotions. We set prices but miss the Value of things and ourselves. We believe in the stories of who we are but never get in touch with our Essence. We know Others through their social portfolios, not empathetic resonance. We vote for our leaders based on promises, not character. We are obsessed with changing the world without understanding the symbiosis. In a nutshell, we freeze the past, frame the future, and fail the present. We are the *Fear culture*."

PanRoo then pauses and looks at the two drinking mentors for validation.

LeDrun, with a smile on his face and tears in his eyes, stows his purple crystal flask inside his shell and turns to Mr. B.V.: "Care for your last masterpiece?"

"Absolutely," Mr. B.V. grins with his signature teeth. He clears his throat and rhymes:

the cat tells a jingle story using AI
she promises the little ones
they will become stars in the virtual sky
the porcupine warns her to either keep her promise or die

thanks to the Love Balloon, the cat flies high
looking at the stats, her Love ends; numbers explain why
past and future debate, the dog and cat vie
the roo hops in; stories told by Fear culture often lie
replacing Truth with Reality, the Virus … the Virus
I ran out of rhyming words, good-bye

"Brahhaha!" LeDrun laughs playfully. "I bet you miss the Origin, where we rarely rely on words for anything. We have Energy, the Universal Language. Be patient, my buddy. We are almost there. Let me see if I can chant one more time."

Before the wise tortoise can utter his chant, the Fear Bubble submerges into the depths of crater lake. As if there were a powerful black hole at the bottom of the lake, the animals are sucked into the center of the tornadic current and lose consciousness.

29
Inside, Screens, Outside

THE ANIMALS OPEN their eyes on the stage of an amphitheater in a park. A band next to them performs meditation music for a yoga dance performing artist in the center of the stage. PanRoo recognizes the splash pad and the large mushroom fountain where Polisco bumped his head. Polisco discerns the public bathroom where his answering of Nature's call was startled by his panicked partner and other strangers. BarKockalotte sees the old battlefield in the park where he was attacked and almost blinded. The young animals become nervous and excited as they appear on stage with an audience. Purrplexy, however, still focuses on the screens without realizing any environmental change.

BarKockalotte is in shock. "How did we get here?" he asks. "This is the sociosphere of LeDrun's workplace. That crater lake must be a Death Portal. But how? I thought the lake was in the **I** Resort where Love Balloons fly. Are they somehow connected? Well, everything is interconnected in the cosmos. Purrplexy! For bone's sake, get your eyes off the damn screens. Look around. Your Fear Bubble took us to the Death Messenger's **D** Lair."

"What are you barking about?" says Purrplexy, taking off her in-ear headphones. "Move your ugly dog face out of the way. You are blocking my vision. I have a new data report to read."

"Vision?" BarKockalotte questions. "What kind of vision prohibits you from seeing your surroundings? In Nature, do wildebeests need data reports to sense the approaching lions? Do studs need data reports to smell available bitche—female dogs?"

"Nonsense," Purrplexy yawns, blinking her dry eyes. "We are not talking about primitive animal instincts. We are talking about advanced civilization. My data reports are much more substantial than any senses or dog barks."

"Something is missing," says PanRoo, looking at the screens and then the amphitheater audience. "BarKockalotte embraces *True experiences* through Energy dynamics between the Self and Others. Purrplexy believes *Real information* selected and rendered before her through the screens. I don't know what to call it, but something Essential is missing through the screens."

"A lot of things are missing, I'm afraid," says Polisco. "First, we experience things all at once in all dimensions—sound, vision, smell, touch, taste, distance, speed, direction, vibe, frequency, force, magnitude, message, intent, sensation, Love, Fear, Energy, Essence. But no matter how advanced our media technologies are, including AI, they are unable to convey a True life experience all at once. The virtual Reality we use the screens to construct has grave limitations. We use words but can only utter one syllable or type one letter at a time, not to mention the arbitrary pronunciations and indoctrinated meanings. We use audio, but the sounds miss their tones and timbres, and voices lose breath. We use images, but they are two-dimensional captures of moments that reduce and freeze-frame the all-dimensional random chaotic waves and patterns of life in real time. We use motion pictures, but we can neither savor the sensational flavors nor touch the rich qualities that a True experience offers. Second, the **F** animals are not Truthful. We deceive, we mislead, and we lie. We lie to Others as well as to the Self. Since Energy is the Universal Language that does not deceive, we use other signals to carry our deceptions—words, numbers, acts, images, motion pictures, and whatnot. Even the past and future are a form of illusion. Among all the tools we adopt to deceive, the screens best serve the purpose to the point that animals like Purrplexy tend to mistake virtual Reality for True life experiences. Third, the platforms that provide the screens are too powerful. It is easy for them to abuse the power to mediate the information we receive to manipulate public opinions and sensations. For instance, our ... "

Purrplexy interrupts Polisco's speech. "That's offensive," she says. "I am not the one who mistakes the screens for Real life. You are! You watch sports games and wear team jerseys under the illusion that you are an athletic sportsbear. You play video games and kill excessively under the illusion that you are a heroic warrior. You watch the news and read about scandals under the illusion that you are a well-informed citizen. You learn positions from porn under the illusion tha—"

Polisco hurriedly stops the uncouth cat. "No illusion in that department! I partially admit what you said. But I have been self-cultivating out of the screen illusions. You, however, use the screens to block the Self from the environing Others. Look around. This is not your Love Balloon anymore. It is the classic Purrplexy two-way glass Fear Bubble, in which Others can see you, but you don't see Others. You use the screens instead to know the Love Value of what you Give. How do you Love inside a Fear Bubble?"

"Speaking of inside," PanRoo asks, "are the screens we use daily considered inside or outside of us?"

"Outside," says BarKockalotte, tilting his head. "These screens report everything that happened outside and around us—what's in the news, what went viral, who said what, who did which, who won, who lost, who slept with—I mean, everything happened out there."

"Inside," Purrplexy argues against the dog. "Look around. My screens are inside. They are an integral part of my life. They schedule all my meetings and vacations, plan my next meals and workouts, alarm me to get up and go to bed, remind me of important dates and to take my pills, assist me at work and entertain me at home, capture my pretty face and social gatherings, share them with all my followers and fans, host video calls with animals for work and with my boyfriend for se—fun activities, so on and so forth. These screens are extensions of my physical body and intelligent mind. They are my internal executive assistant."

"The screens cannot experience life for us," says PanRoo, gazing at the wall of screens, "thus they are neither your body nor your mind, neither inside nor outside. I believe they are in the middle. Maybe that's why they are called the media."

"The screens do not provide True life experiences," says Polisco, gazing at the wall of screens, "but they construct a virtual Reality that consumes our Energy. Love Energy interplays between the Self and Others and generates new experiences for both at present. Fear Energy repels Others to preserve the Self of the past and future. The screens insert themselves between the past and future to replace the present. Do you know what else is in the middle? The Virus."

"Are you saying the virtual Reality is the Viral Reality?" BarKockalotte barks with shocked eyes.

"Not quite," Polisco explains, pressing his face against the glass wall to check the stage and audience. "But I think the virtual Reality could serve as a ramp, a boarding bridge, or a slippery slope to the Viral Reality if it separates Essence from Identity, such as Purrplexy's purrsona stories. They exemplify the *separation* between who she Truly is and what she Gives. Where there is a rupture between Essence and Identity, there is a culture for the Virus."

"Says who!" Purrplexy demands. "The polar bear who wants to use robots to cheer up his customers? Is there any rupture between who you Truly are and what you Give? Take a close look at your Self before you start running your mouth about Others. Ironically, we made a jingle for your cheerleader robots that have not been in production yet, but I did not see you stopping us. Does it make you a hypocrite?"

Polisco's face turns red. He opens his mouth several times but cannot utter a word.

PanRoo quietly reflects to see if she has a rupture between her Essence and Identity. Polisco thinks that she is judging him.

The two senior Messengers wink at each other and smile. Polisco feels that they are mocking him.

BarKockalotte senses the inner turmoil of his polar bear master. He decides to divert the attention.

"Can you explain the environmental change?" BarKockalotte asks Purrplexy. "From high in the sky to the lake, then the park, what is going on in your mind?"

"Surroundings do not concern me," says Purrplexy, reading something on the screen. "I am intrigued by this report on the strong positive correlation between commercials' volume and audience's attention. I want to try it."

"The volume of farts has a strong positive correlation with the victims' attention," BarKockalotte mumbles. "Not all attention is Love attention."

"Let's look at the environment for a second," PanRoo says to Purrplexy, quieting the dog. "The Fear Bubble blocks your immediate, True experience with the environing Others while the screens are building you a virtual Reality. Look at the stage, the musicians and artists, and the audience in the theater. You turn a blind eye to all of them!"

Purrplexy interrupts PanRoo with dilated pupils "There is an audience? Why didn't you all tell me? It is an excellent opportunity to raise our volume and reap more attention! Let me plug in my world-class loudspeakers. Kids! Let's crank up the music and jingle! It's time to Give!"

Purrplexy leads the jingle performance on the stage. The young stars follow her steps. The sudden, appalling jingle, like loud ads, assaults everybody's senses. The enraged artists and audience show their feelings by throwing cellos, harps, violins, flutes, bottles, cans, shoes, stinky eggs, dog poop bags, and other stuff at the enthusiastic Givers. The growing pile floods and buries Purrplexy's Fear Bubble until it's pitch-black inside and outside. The frightened and frustrated young stars start crying. Their feline leader, however, continues Giving her Love Value regardless. In the loud darkness, LeDrun chants:

> *Essential Truth, Viral Reality*
> *Essence and Identity are one*
> *collective Identity convinces unique Essence*
> *past and future converge at present*
> *past and future tell present a popular story*
> *inside message is outside signal and vice versa*
> *inside and outside are mediated by mass media*
> *Give and Receive through Love Bonds*
> *offer and consume via transactions and currency*
> *Love Value mutually fulfills and enriches*
> *massive impact made Real by power and platforms*
> *Essential Legacy lives on and flourishes with Truth*
> *Viral Legend dies and freezes in the record as Reality*

Suddenly, a red beam casts down from the ceiling and travels to every corner of the otherwise dark box. A familiar Voice creeps into everyone's ears: "Welcome back to the stage, my superstar. Your fans are missing you."

30
Return to Natural Legacy

THE ANIMALS STAND inside an enormous red glass box in the middle of a dark world. Various screens on both the inner and outer walls brightly and loudly announce their presence. On the interior screens, the animals see preinstalled apps, icons, logos, symbols, and neatly organized blue folders. At the top and center of the screens, motion-activated cameras blink their red eyes at the performers, ready to capture their camera smiles. Purrplexy is once again petrified as the traumatic memories of what happened last time in this red box flare up.

"Look at the camera, my superstar," says the Voice.

Purrplexy sits still like a cat sculpture.

The children smile at the cameras like four rising stars.

"Thank you," the Voice laughs. "Your time will come, I promise. This space is dedicated to our superstar—Purrplexy. So, please look into any camera to unlock your legendary future."

Steam and smoke seep from the cat sculpture's

mouth, nostrils, eyes, and ears. She is burning up inside. BarKockalotte forces some ice water into her mouth and raises her chin toward the camera. All the screens suddenly brighten up. On the east screen are stats and rankings of the educational institutions and academic majors. On the west screen are data and lists of hot industries and career paths. On the north screen are line graphs and pie charts of dominant fashions, entertainment, and lifestyles. And on the south screen are famous names and their Legends. In the center of the floor are two red sofas and a coffee table on a stage for an interview with the superstar. The Voice on the right side of the sofa hosts the show.

The Voice introduces Purrplexy. "Ladies and gentlemen, I give you the superstar!"

"I am on TV!" Joecub darts out for the interviewee's red sofa.

"It is a trap! It is a trap! It is a trap!" Purrplexy wakes up from the trance and warns the child. "The monster will burn you out from the inside! Stay True to your Self and Others!"

"Don't listen to my crazy cat fan," says Joecub, sitting on the sofa. "I am honored to be on TV."

"We are honored to have you," says the Voice. "So, what is your story?"

Joecub introduces himself: "I am a schooler," he begins. "My daddy and mommy have a business. We have a dog and a cat. They fight a lot."

"Yeah, yeah," says the Voice impatiently. "You know what a story is? It is your show filled with conflicts, drama, twists, pains, joys, romance, and violence. Simply, your story is what you Give to the world."

"Does it have to be True?" Joecub asks.

"Between True and popular, it is your choice," says the Voice.

"I choose popular!" Joecub says without hesitation.

"Excellent choice!" says the Voice. "So, what is your story?"

Joecub looks at his parents and the other animals, thinks for a while, and begins telling his story. "I am an orphan. My dad was a business bear. He was killed in a mass shooting. My mom was an immigrant who killed herself due to depression. Then, a beaver grandpa adopted me. We have a dog and a cat. The dog was born into a criminal family. His dad and brothers were all killed in a prison riot, but he is a police dog. The cat is very sick with something called Star Syndrome, so we started a charitable foundation to help all cats with illnesses."

"Wrong! Not True! Liar! Thief! What the heck?" the insulted animals protest against Joecub's stolen story.

"Extraordinary!" the Voice praises Joecub. "What is your future Legend?"

"I don't know," Joecub shrugs. "I am just a cub. I have not written my future story yet."

"Fair enough," says the Voice. "Same question: Do you choose Truth or popularity?"

"Popularity!" Joecub shouts with a big smile.

Now the Voice raises its volume. "Then the future Legend has been written for you!" Do you see the screens? They are Real scripts tested and endorsed by the majority, the masses—the soil for popularity. All you need to do is check some boxes, make some choices from the scripts, and then fabricate them into your own story to Give. I promise you popularity and stardom."

"Let's do that!" says Joecub, checking out some life choices on the screen.

"Congratulations!" the Voice shouts. "A superstar is born! So, what is your ending?"

Joecub sits back on the red sofa and crosses his legs with contentment. "What ending?"

"Every story has an ending," says the Voice.

"I'll choose a superstar ending," says Joecub, gazing at the screen.

The Voice applauds. "Bravo! Your story might not be True, but all your choices are Real. They will be recorded under your name. It is your Legend! Now, let's take the last shot."

A gun appears on the coffee table.

"Execute it!" the Voice commands.

Joecub picks up the gun and aims at his little cub head.

"No!" Purrplexy yells. She jumps onto the stage, grabs the gun from Joecub's paw, and throws it at the Voice.

The bear parents dash to the red sofa and carry their cub off the stage.

"Ouch," the Voice moans. "Take a seat, superstar."

Purrplexy takes a deep breath, summons all her courage, and sits down to face her Virus.

"What is your story?" the Voice asks.

"Do you want a True story or a popular one?" Purrplexy asks.

"It is your life," says the Voice. "It is your choice. But who does not want to be popular? Popularity makes you feel safe, powerful, Loved, Valued, well-connected. After all, we are social animals."

"I choose a True story," says Purrplexy with a long exhale. "Popularity neither springs from my Essence nor embodies my Identity. Thus, it is not my story."

"But it could become your Legend," the Voice persists. "Popularity may not contain Truth, but it is a type of Reality. As long as your name is written in this Reality, you will pass it down from generation to generation. You will be remembered, revered, quoted, maybe even studied."

"Even if my story is not True?" asks Purrplexy.

"Nobody cares," the Voice laughs. "How many Realities are group fictions?"

"We care," PanRoo says, holding Joecub tightly. "The type of Reality you talk about is Viral Reality. The first slippery slope to the Viral Reality is *separation* so that the Virus can build its Power Center in the rupture. In Purrplexy's case, it is the separation of *Truth* from *Reality*, thus the Essence from Identity, the Self from Others, and the Legacy from Legend. In Nature's Sphere, Legacy and Legend are one. Legacy is what you Give from your Essence to Others through Love that influences them, generates anew with their Essence, and flourishes in both. It carries your Essence and thrives in Others. Legend is your Legacy narrated by Others as your story that honors the past and motivates the future. However, in Viral Reality, unique life narratives are often reduced to mass-produced stories."

"Where there is no Legacy, but everyone is a Legend," says LeDrun, sipping his purple crystal flask.

"Second, *replacement*," Polisco continues. "Taking advantage of the separation, the Social Virus inculcates more artificial social inventions to replace Legacy—fame, stardom, fandom, persona, profile, resume, publicity, promotion, advertisement, campaign, and more. Take the F animals' screen life as an example. Advertisements have replaced adventure and encounter; entertainment replaced connection and cocreation; news replaced events and happenings; images replaced moments; videos replaced interaction; profiles replaced characters; offers replaced Value, and so forth. It is an artificial construct where life is a show on various screens. Once separated and replaced, the Virus successfully settles in the victim's mind for further indoctrination and exploitation."

BarKockalotte woofs his illumination. "Third, *Power*. The Virus then invites Power to accelerate the slippery slope into the Viral Reality. Power is the judgment of influence—massive or minute, fast or slow, deep or shallow, significant or insignificant, popular or unpopular, famous or unknown, dramatic or inconsequential, game-changing or unnoticeable. The primary role of Viral Power is to reorient its subjects by telling them where they should concentrate their Energy—Fear Energy, of course, because Love neither separates nor judges. Love bonds and cocreates. At this point, the Social Virus has finished building its Power Center to lord over its victims."

"To disguise Fear as Love," Purrplexy ponders on the red sofa, "the monster's ultimate lure. The last slippery slope to the Viral Reality is the *pursuit of Power*. In Nature's Sphere, Love and Fear flow in harmony—*Love gives way to Fear when in danger; Fear gives way to Love when safe.* In my Viral Reality, it is the pursuit of popularity, which incurs nothing but atrophy. *Rich is a Natural growth experience;*

Poor is a Virus conditioned mindset. Unlearn to save the children."

Purrplexy stands up, picks up the gun from the host's sofa and starts shooting at the screens on the walls of her two-way glass box. Soon the screens are shattered, the walls dissolved, the inside illumed.

"BORN RICH LEARN POOR," says Mr. B.V., smiling at Purrplexy. "You were born with tremendous Love Value to Give. Return to your Natural Legacy. I am about to return, too."

PURRPLEXY OPENS HER eyes at gunpoint. The big porcupine has returned to collect the debt incurred by her earlier promise. BarKockalotte pulls back the slingshot to maximum draw tension, aiming at the big porcupine and barking his final warnings. Polisco holds a stun gun in one paw and uses the other paw to protect Joecub. PanRoo holds pepper spray with both paws and shields the little raccoon behind her. Mr. B.V. holds his grandson tightly in his arms. LeDrun retracts inside his shell.

"Don't shoot! Brother!" the little porcupine pushes his brother's arm and pleads. "I don't want to be a star!"

"It is not up to you!" the big porcupine yells. "Get off my arm before you get hurt!"

"There will be no company jingle," Purrplexy says calmly. "It is cancelled because it does not tell the True story."

"I don't care!" The big porcupine aims his gun between

the cat's eyes. "A promise is a promise. Give me the money or give me your life."

Purrplexy stares resolutely at the big porcupine. "My life is not for me to Give or for you to take."

"Let's see," says the big porcupine. He pulls the trigger. "No!"

All the animals jump on the thorny shooter. The little porcupine stabs him in the arm with his barbs. The polar bear stuns him in the chest with his stun gun. The panda kangaroo sprays him in the eyes with her pepper spray. The dog shoots him in the head with his slingshot. The little cub and the little raccoon scream like sirens. The shooter is down, and the cat's life has been saved, thanks to the rescue squad. As the animals breathe a sigh of relief, the little beaver, shivering and covered with blood, crawls out from under Mr. B.V.'s body and cries, "My grandpa has been shot."

31
Beyond Life and Death

MR. B.V. LIES in bed in the hospital emergency room. His eyes are tightly closed, mouth slightly open. The monitors next to him have all fallen flat like broken arrows that have lost their nocks and points to life. The rest of the animals mourn, some silently and some loudly, when a doctor comes out bearing the heartbreakingly tragic news in the hallway. They are allowed into the room one by one to say their final goodbyes. Mr. B.V.'s grandkit goes in first.

"Grandpa B.V. or whoever you are," the little beaver sobs, "I want to thank you for saving me from that bad grandpa. You turned him from a cold mean beaver to a warm wise grandpa, actually more like a grandma. Anyway, you must have played magic on his heart. I understand you have to go and save other kids from bad grandpas, but I am very sad to say goodbye. Do you think Joecub's grandma, or his parents will let me stay with them? I like them a lot.

I mean, I did not like them in the beginning, but I think they had a change of heart too. It must be your magic."

While the little beaver is kissing his grandpa goodbye on the forehead, he perceives a greyish giant hologram rising up out of the dead beaver body and giving him a heartwarming embrace.

"Wise Teeth," Polisco calls Mr. B.V., sitting at the bedside, "it really sucked that the doctors couldn't bring you back, but what you did to protect your grandkit was heroic. The porcupine shooter is in custody now. He will probably join his thorny father and prickly brother soon, given the prison situation on planet F. Listen, I want to thank you for guiding me through those slippery slopes down into my Viral Reality when I have tried to discover my Essence with Others. You are Nature's Messenger, so I know you can hear this Message of gratitude over your seemingly dead body. In Reality, you die. In Truth, you transform. Transform in peace, my friend. We will carry on your Legacy."

Polisco stands up to leave and then pauses as if he forgot something. He looks around stealthily, sticks his giant bear paw under the sheet, and begins fishing around. "Smack!" Polisco's face swells up immediately as he receives an overwhelming slap. With blurry vision and a slight concussion, the polar bear perceives an angry greyish giant hologram with large breasts.

"Mr. B.V.," PanRoo wipes the tears off her dark eye circles with both paws, "I was paralyzed when the doctor told us that you had passed away. I felt that a part of me went with you. But as I sit here and look at you, I know that it is not a part of me that went with you; it is a part of you that is staying with me. Thank you for cultivating me through the slippery slopes down into my Viral Reality when I have tried to liberate my Essence with Others. I know you are getting the Message. As a Messenger, the beaver is one of your endless embodiments. You probably need to return to the Origin for your Life Lab. Don't worry. We will care for your grandkit and the other children, including the little porcupine. I know, in Reality you die, but in Truth you return. Return in peace, my friend. We will carry on your Legacy."

PanRoo stands up to leave, pausing as if she too left something behind. She carefully checks the room and finds a bag that contains Mr. B.V.'s belongings. Unzipping the bag, PanRoo sticks her right arm in and starts fishing around. "Peng! Kwuh!" There is an explosion inside the sack. PanRoo is blown onto the wall and hits the floor. As she picks herself up and limps out, the panda kangaroo discerns a watchful greyish giant hologram hovering just beneath the ceiling.

"Wake up! Wake up!" BarKockalotte barks with tears shooting out. "Don't you have magic powers? How can you die? Wake up, please!" The dog then lies down next to Mr. B.V.'s body. "I know you are not dead," he says, sniffing the beaver. "The decaying smell must come from your beaver Identity, not your Messenger Essence. You are immortal because of your Love Bonds with many mortals like me. I want to thank you for illuminating the slippery slopes down into my Viral Reality when I have tried to grow Rich with Others. I know, in Reality you die, but in Truth you continue on. Continue in peace, my friend. We will carry on your Legacy."

BarKockalotte jumps off the bed to leave, then returns. "I am wondering," he says, "when and where we could see you again. Your Life Lab? LeDrun's **D** Lair? Jo and I are excellent jugglers now, thanks to you. Maybe the three of us could host a juggling exhibition with all kinds of balls and drink some elixir punch ... the elixir ... " The dog starts snuffling around in the room. As he detects something under the bed and sticks his head in for further investigation, a greyish giant's hand reaches out from under Mr. B.V.'s sheet, drags the dog out by his tail, and throws him out the door.

"I didn't believe you could die," Purrplexy meows, sitting atop the highest monitor. "That's why I could stand up against the violent porcupine. You gave me the courage and strength. Had I foreseen this collateral damage ... but we cannot truly predict what will happen in the future or go back to the past to change what happened. Even if we could, I probably would do the same thing. So, my question is: How dare you leave us when your mission to cultivate us into new Messengers is incomplete? I know I am not the smartest in the family, but I do want to say thank you for enlightening me on all the slippery slopes down into my Viral Reality when I have tried to cocreate my Legacy with Others. I am not in my two-way glass Fear Bubble right now. I see Others. I see you. You may change to a different orbit under a different name or form, but you won't die. I mean, in Reality you die, but in Truth you change. Change in peace, my friend. We will carry on your Legacy."

As Purrplexy is about to jump off the monitor to leave, she recalls something important. She turns around and carefully inspects the crevice between the monitors and the wall as if she were stalking magic. A greyish giant arm reaches out through the screen, scuffs the cat, and throws her out of the window.

"Mr. B.V.!" Joecub crawls onto the beaver's death bed and shakes the dead body. The bear cub then fishes around in his little pocket and takes out a purple crystal flask. He places the flask on the pillow with tremendous care as if he were handling a newborn life and whispers into the beaver's ear: "Mr. B.V., I am sorry that I stole your magic bottle from the Life Lab. You were juggling two magic bottles but missed the purple one. I wanted to have magic powers like you so I could beat the mind monster that eats children's brains. But it is empty! I dare not tell anybody. They would ground me and take my magic bottle away. If you were alive, you would hear that right now the four adults outside are fighting about who should get your magic bottle, the green one, if they could find it. Sometimes I think if the adults talked less they would have a better chance of catching their mind monster. Anyway, I want to tell you that I feel really, really bad. Had I not taken your magic bottle, you would have had more magic power to fight against the big porcupine. But then again, the bottle was empty. How do you fill it with elix-sir?"

The beaver's body disappears. A green crystal flask appears on the pillow, next to the purple one.

"Mr. B.V.?!" Joecub is startled and scared. He holds the two magic bottles tightly to his chest and looks around in a fluster.

"Mr. B.V. has returned to the Origin," says LeDrun, appearing on the pillow. "I will do the same because we have accomplished our mission. Nature now has four new

Messengers on planet **F**. Our Life Lab and **D** Lair are waiting for us. It is time to return."

"What about me?" asks Joecub, shedding tears. "The mind monster will eat my brain. I see it everywhere. It is scary!"

LeDrun smiles, comforting the bear cub. "Your family will take care of you."

"But the mind monster looks just like them," the child murmurs. "What about the two magic bottles?" Joecub works a different angle. "Could I return to the Origin with you? I'd like to put them back in Mr. B.V.'s paws and say sorry."

"You can trust me with them," says LeDrun.

"No," says Joecub, shielding the two magic bottles from the tortoise. "You have a bit of a drinking problem."

"They are empty!" LeDrun rolls his eyes and raises his claws. Like magnets, the two crystal flasks are sucked out of the little bear's paws and into the Death Messenger's claws.

Losing his bargaining chips, the bear cub throws a lethal and suicidal tantrum.

LeDrun swiftly exchanges a smile with the greyish giant behind the monitors. He places the two flasks back to the cub's paws to quiet down the screaming child. He then crosses his legs, closes his eyes, and says to Joecub: "Put your little paw on my chest button. Let's return."

In a split second, the emergency room is empty.

32
The Sanctuary

THE ORIGIN IS where everything originates and returns. Shapes emerge and disappear. Patterns form and dissolve. Boundaries appear and vanish. Waves collapse as they are observed. It is embodied by a greyish sphere that embraces symbiotically manifold unique Essence and constantly flowing universal Energy. Everything returns to nothing. Nothing gives rise to everything. Joecub swims like a fish in the endless ocean and flies like a bird in the limitless sky. He lets go of what he has learned from the adult **F** animals and sees the unlearned yet omniscient Essence of himself. Following LeDrun, he enters the newly restored Life Lab where PaGoo is juggling air.

"Jo," says LeDrun to the bear cub, "now you can return the flasks and say sorry."

"Under one condition," Joecub negotiates.

"What is that?" LeDrun exchanges a quick smile with PaGoo.

Now Joecub reveals his true intention. "Let me stay here," he says. "I would do anything to avoid going back to that planet."

"You cannot stay here, my child," says PaGoo, raising her giant hands to retrieve the two flasks from Joecub. Like magnets, the two crystal flasks again are sucked out of the little bear's paws. The Life Messenger waves the flasks and continues: "If you insist, I can mix and mingle your Essence with the whole cosmic Essence of Others for a new life on a new journey. However, in that case, on planet **F**, to those who know you as Joecub, you will be dead in Reality."

"What is the difference?" Joecub cries. "On planet **F**, everybody gets killed by other animals or themselves. They make me go to school, but there are a lot of shootings on campus. Even if I do not get shot at school, I have to spend many years there studying things important to them, not to us. I don't know which is worse—getting shot or getting schooled. Even if I survive, the mind monster will eat my brain alive. When brainless, I will become its believer and eat other animals' brains. I would rather die. Can you turn me into a bird or fish in a better place?"

"What about your family?" asks LeDrun with deep concern. "They will be heartbroken over your death."

"They have introduced the mind monster to me," says Joecub in pain. "My dad wants me to win. My mom trains me to fit in. Mr. Bar encourages me to Have and Have more. Purrplexy shows me how to Give for popularity on the screen. Then they all say they Love me. I think their Love is Fear in disguise."

"Jo," PaGoo sighs, "I am truly sorry. I will grant your wish for a rebirth. But before I give you a new life path, do you want to send a Message to your family? They are all Messengers now. They can receive it instantly."

Joecub thinks for a while and says: "Daddy, Mommy, Mr. Bar, and Lexy, I am scared. I think I have caught your mind monster in my head. It wants my brain. It shows up in my dreams, at home, at school, on TV and smart phones, my toys, my clothes, everywhere. I cannot escape. I do not want to grow up with the mind monster, but I do not know how to grow up by myself. So, I must end it for good."

All four adults appear in the Life Lab upon receiving the Message. The shocked and puzzled child hides behind PaGoo's giant leg pylon.

"They are all Nature's Messengers now," says LeDrun to Joecub. "That is to say, they know how to beat the Social Virus, i.e., the mind monster. You will be safe with them. And most importantly, they know how to make Love Bonds with Others for cocreation and cogrowth. They are Rich."

The four green Messengers look at Joecub with hopeful, tearful eyes.

"Only if LeDrun comes with me," Joecub demands, peeking out from behind PaGoo's leg.

"Absolutely!" PaGoo winks at LeDrun. "He said you were the key!"

LeDrun gives PaGoo a big side-eye.

POLISCO COMES HOME from the foster care agency with the little beaver and porcupine. The two children kick off their round leather shoes, hang their ballistic helmets on the wall, and peel off their bulletproof overalls. They sniff each other with immense excitement and dash out to the backyard to join their new bear brother and raccoon sister. Polisco picks a wedgie, scratches an itch down there, and, with ephemeral contentment, sniffs his stubby paw fingers in a quasi-rock-and-roll gesture. The polar bear Messenger then conjures up a purple crystal flask

and saunters into the sunroom.

PanRoo meditates in the sunroom. The bamboo leaves outside the bay window ride the sunlight and wind, gently swaying on her round and peaceful face. A fluffy and flavored polar bear paw holding a purple crystal flask moves under PanRoo's nose. As she inhales, Love Energy carries Polisco's Love Message. It permeates around and resonates within PanRoo to form the fulfilling Love Bond that fills both crystal flasks with elixir.

"All done?" PanRoo asks, taking a green crystal flask from her pouch.

"All done." Polisco sits next to his partner.

"I have been meditating," says PanRoo, sipping her green elixir, "on the Sanctuary where the Rich live and thrive. Reflecting on the journey of Self-discovery, liberation, and cultivation, we know that *Rich is a Natural growth experience* during which our Love Balloons bond with many other Love Balloons to resonate, reflect, cocreate, and mutually enrich. I wonder if the Sanctuary is *not a place* but *a State*—a Natural State where Love is safe to bond and grow."

"Natural State versus Viral Mindset," says Polisco, guzzling his purple elixir, "Rich or Poor at whim. The Viral Reality is fabricated with social inventions and group fictions and then gets indoctrinated in our minds as Reality without Truth. The Poor dedicate their life Energy to learning, believing, exemplifying, and continuing the fabrication. The Sanctuary is a Natural State that springs from our intrinsic Essence and radiates out through our Energy to bond and cocreate. The Rich entangle their unique Essence and universal Energy with Others with mutual respect, resonance, inspiration, and enrichment to cocreate a symbiotic community."

"My fellow Messenger," says PanRoo, looking at Polisco, "where do we start on this infected planet to offer such a Sanctuary?"

"I think it has already started," says Polisco, looking outside the window.

OUTSIDE THE WINDOW in the backyard, LeDrun meditates under the maple tree. It is late fall. All the leaves have consummated their life cycle and returned to the root. Layers of red palmy leaves under the tree weave a natural red carpet for the Death Messenger to return. The little bear, together with his raccoon sister, porcupine brother, and beaver brother, encircles the meditating tortoise. BarKockalotte sploots on the red leaves. Purrplexy leans against him, tucking her paws.

"LeDrun," says Joecub, raising his paw, "where is the Sanctuary? I heard that it is a safe and Rich place without the brain-eating mind monster. What does it look like? Can we go?"

"Grass green. Cat Purr," LeDrun answers with eyes

closed. "Jo, that was what you said under the tree before you were introduced to the mind monster. Unlearn and return to Rich, my child."

Purrplexy purrs, responding to the cue as a new Nature's Messenger:

> the Sanctuary
> safe and Rich
> a Natural State
> not a destination place

"What State?" the little raccoon asks. "Like a country? Is it United?"

"Probably a Natural State of being," BarKockalotte woofs. "A safe State that Love bonds and Essence shows."

"I did not feel safe with my dad and brothers," says the little porcupine, "but I feel safe with my new parents."

"I do not feel safe at school," says the little beaver, "but I feel safe at my new home."

"I do not feel safe in Star Valley," says the little raccoon, "but I feel safe with my new family."

"I do not feel safe on this planet," says Joecub, crossing his arms, "but I feel safe now because LeDrun is here. He has a magic bottle that gives him magic powers. I used to have a magic bottle too. But it was empty. What is your secret for refilling your bottle?"

"Fish swim. Birds fly," says LeDrun, quoting Joecub again before he was introduced to the mind monster. "Unlearn and return to Rich, my child."

"The dog barks up the right tree," BarKockalotte cues himself as a new Nature's Messenger:

the Sanctuary
a Natural State
Rich is to enrich mutually
fulfill together
not refill alone

"I don't understand," says Joecub with a frown.

"It means that the elixir is from your Love Bond," says PanRoo, coming out of the sunroom with Polisco and sitting down to join the circle. "The Virus consumes you. The Sanctuary fulfills you."

The children shake their heads.

"Do you feel safe at this moment under the tree?" Polisco asks.

"Yes," the children nod.

"That is the beginning of the Sanctuary," BarKockalotte woofs.

"Put your paws on my chest button," Purrplexy meows, revealing a round, half-green-half-purple, yin yang button. "Let us take a Love Balloon journey together."

"Return to Rich," LeDrun smiles, opening his eyes to take one last look.

Epilogue

LᴇDʀᴜɴ ʟɪᴇs ɪɴ the bloody red palmy leaves, surrounded by his beloved animals. The Death Messenger has begun his journey of return. His Essence rises up above his body and floats away as he forgets about being a tortoise. All the **F** words evaporate into thin air. All the **F** knowledge sinks into the earth. He unlearns everything acquired in the **F** society so that his Essence is free to return. The tortoise's body is drenched with tears as the strong waves of Love crash upon the shores of the eyes of the beholders. The morning sky illuminates. The Sanctuary germinates under the tree. LeDrun perches on the lowest bare branch and chants with his last breath:

a civilized wasteland
Love is mistaken
Fear feeds the Virus
unlearn, return
the Poor become Rich again
being and interbeing
the Sanctuary, cocreation

Eight pairs of paws, inch by inch, dig a resting place under the maple tree for the tortoise, where he meditated and practiced his Tai Chi. The Messengers pour all the elixir around the grave and place his purple crystal flask atop as his tombstone. "Essential Observer, Eternal Legacy," says the epitaph.

NATURE IS TORN. She is bright about the new Messengers and yet gloomy about the vast majority of the infected animals that remain on planet **F**. Upon receiving her cosmic Message, the four new Messengers gather together at the speed of thought for an emergency meeting.

"My new Messengers," says Nature, "I am excited about your enlightenment yet exhausted by planet **F**. I bestow all my children on planet **F** with fresh air, but they have polluted it; wholesome nourishment but they contaminated it; a rich diversity of Essence but they conformed it; and creative Love and protective Fear but they abused both. They have turned the Sanctuary into a Factory that exploits me to feed the Virus. I summoned you here to ask you a question. Are you willing to work for me like LeDrun and PaGoo so that I can clear planet **F** with the reset button?"

"What if," Purrplexy asks, "we carry on LeDrun and PaGoo's Legacy by continuing the Messenger cultivation program? We have four young aspiring candidates at home. We are not going to abandon the children."

"Yes," says BarKockalotte. "Their Love has been rekindled. They are ready to discover their Essence.

Together, we can build a Sanctuary, a Virus-free State on this infected planet, a safe State for Love to grow."

Nature smiles and asks: "You are willing to be the seed that preserves me among this unsustainable civilization?"

"The Virus has its colonies," says Polisco. "We have our Sanctuary. The Virus is self-destructive, thus the unsustainable civilization."

"The Sanctuary is cocreative," says PanRoo, "thus the ever-growing Legacy."

"Shall we?" the Messengers behold Nature.

THE END AND BEGINNING

Made in the USA
Columbia, SC
09 February 2025

53110407R00157